New York Time… r
Katee Rob…
grandpa's kn… *t*
was a RITA®…
it 'a compulsiv… ght
amount of susp… hot writing
sexy contempor… suspense she spends
her time playing …ve games with her children,
driving her husband batty with *what-if?* questions,
and planning for the inevitable zombie apocalypse.

If you liked *Make Me Want*, why not try

Sweet Thing by Nicola Marsh
My Royal Temptation by Riley Pine
Ruined by Jackie Ashenden

MAKE ME WANT

KATEE ROBERT

MILLS & BOON

First Published in Great Britain 2018
by Mills & Boon, an imprint of HarperCollins*Publishers*
1 London Bridge Street, London, SE1 9GF

ISBN: 978-0-263-93210-2

MIX
Paper from
responsible sources
FSC C007454

This book is produced from independently certified FSC™ paper
to ensure responsible forest management.
For more information visit www.harpercollins.co.uk/green.

Printed and bound in Spain
by CPI, Barcelona

To Tim.

Second chances make for the best stories.

CHAPTER ONE

GIDEON NOVAK had almost canceled the meeting. He would have if he'd possessed even a shred of honor. Some things in this world were just too damn good for him to be associated with and Lucy Baudin topped that list. To hear from her now, two years after...

Focus on the facts.

She'd called. He'd answered. It was as simple as that.

The law office of Parker and Jones was the same as it had been the last time he'd walked through the doors. The small army of defense attorneys took on mostly white-collar crimes—specifically the ones that paid well—and that showed in every element of the interior. Soothing colors and bold lines projected confidence and created a calming effect.

Pale blue walls and good lines didn't do a single damn thing to dial back the pressure building in his chest with each step.

He usually didn't contract out with law offices. As a headhunter, Gideon preferred to stick to tech companies, various start-up corporations or, literally, anyone except lawyers. They were too controlling and wanted their hands on every detail, every step of the way. It was a pain in the ass.

This is for Lucy.

He kept his expression schooled on the elevator ride up. When he'd known her, she was somewhere around floor six, proving herself by working cases not big enough for the lawyers with seniority to want but that were too big to turn down. Now she was on floor nineteen, only a couple below Parker and Jones themselves. She'd done well for herself in the two years since he'd seen her last. Really well.

The elevator opened into a large waiting room that didn't look anything like an actual waiting room. The more money people had, the more care was required in handling them, and the coffee bar and scattering of couches and trade magazines reflected that. The hallway was guarded by a large desk and an older woman with tasteful gray shot through her dark hair. Surprising. He'd expected a bottle-blond receptionist—or perhaps a brunette if they were feeling adventurous.

But then the woman looked up and he got the impression of a general surveying her domain. *Ah.* They'd chosen someone who couldn't be bulldozed, if he didn't miss his guess. Useful to keep unruly clients in line.

Gideon stopped in front of the desk and did his best to appear nonthreatening. "I'm here to see Lucy Baudin."

"She's expecting you." She turned back to her computer, effectively dismissing him.

He spent half a second wondering at her qualifications—and if she was amiable to being poached for a different company—before he set it aside. Stepping on Lucy's toes by stealing her receptionist wasn't a good way to start off this meeting.

He'd spent the last week trying to figure out why the hell Lucy would seek *him* out. New York was rife with headhunters. Gideon was good—better than good—but considering their history, there had to be someone better suited for the job.

You could have said no.

Yeah, he could have.

But he owed Lucy Baudin. A single meeting wasn't much in the face of the fact that he'd more or less single-handedly brought her engagement down in flames.

He knocked on the dark wooden door as he opened it. The office was bright and airy, big windows overlooking New York, the only furniture a large L-shaped desk and two comfortable-looking chairs arranged in front of it. Gideon took in the room in a single sweep and then focused on the woman behind the desk.

Lucy sat straight, her narrow shoulders tense, as if she was about to step onto a battlefield. Her long dark hair was pinned back into some style that looked effortless but probably took a significant amount of time to accomplish. She raised her pointed chin, which drew his attention to her mouth. Lucy's features were a little too sharp to pass for traditional beauty—she would have made a killing on a runway—but her mouth was full and generous and had always been inclined to smile.

There were no smiles today.

"Lucy." He shut the door behind him, holding his place to let her guide the interaction. She was the one who'd called him here. It didn't feel natural to take his lead from someone else, but for her he'd make an effort.

At least until he heard her out.

"Gideon. Sit, please." She motioned at the chairs in front of the desk.

Maybe she could pretend this was like any other job interview, but he couldn't stop staring at her. She wore a dark gray dress that set off her pale skin and dark hair, leaving the only color present in her blue eyes and red lips. It created a striking picture. The woman was a goddamn gift. She always had been.

Jeff, you fucked things up beyond all recognition when you threw her away.

Focus.

She hadn't arranged this meeting because of their past. If she could be professional, then he'd manage, as well. It was the least he could do.

Gideon sank into the chair and leaned forward, bracing his elbows on his knees. "You said this was about a job."

"Yes." A faint blush colored her pale cheeks, highlighting the smattering of freckles there. "This is confidential, of course."

It wasn't quite a question, but he answered it anyway. "I didn't put together a nondisclosure, but I can do that if you need to make it official."

"That won't be necessary. Your word that it stays between us will be enough."

Curiosity curled through him. He'd had clients insist on confidentiality in the past—it was more the rule than the exception—but this felt different. He set the thought aside and focused on the job. "It would help if you'd describe the position you want filled. It gives me a general idea of what you're looking for, and we can narrow it down from there."

She met his gaze directly, her blue eyes startling. "The position I need filled is a husband."

Gideon shook his head, sure he'd heard her wrong. "Excuse me?"

"A husband." She held up her left hand and wiggled her ring finger. "Before you get that look on your face, let me explain."

He didn't have any *look* on his face. *A husband. Where the fuck does she think I'm going to find a husband?* He opened his mouth to ask exactly that, but Lucy beat him there. "The timing isn't ideal, but gossip has come down the grapevine that I'm being considered for partner at the end of the year. While that would normally be a cause for celebration, some of the old guard have very strong beliefs about single women." She rolled her eyes, the first *Lucy* thing he'd seen her do since he'd arrived. "It would be laughable if it wasn't standing in the way of what I want, but I watched Georgia get passed over for a promotion last year for this exact reason. She wouldn't bend and they chose her male competition instead."

She was dead serious.

Gideon took a breath, trying to approach this logically. Obviously she'd put a lot of thought into the idea, and if she was misguided, that didn't mean he had to verbally slap her down. *This* Lucy, put-together and in control, was a far cry from when he'd seen her last, sobbing and broken. But that didn't change the fact that they were one and the same. He could handle this calmly and get her to see reason.

But calm and reasonable wasn't what came out of his mouth. "Are you out of your goddamn mind, Lucy? I'm a headhunter—not a matchmaker. Even if I was, getting married to secure a promotion is bullshit."

"Is it?" She shrugged. "People get married for much less valid reasons. *I* almost married for love before, and we both know how that ended. There's nothing wrong with handling marriage like a business arrangement—plenty of cultures do exactly that."

"We aren't talking about other cultures. We're talking about *you*."

Another shrug. As if it didn't matter to her one way or another. He *loathed* that feigned indifference, but he didn't have a goddamn right to challenge her on it.

She met his gaze directly. "This is important to me, Gideon. I don't know about kids—I love my job, and having babies would potentially interfere with that—but I'm lonely. It wouldn't be so bad to have someone to come home to, even if it wasn't a love for the ages. *Especially* if it's not a love for the ages."

"Lucy, that's crazy." Every word out of her mouth cut into the barrier of professionalism he fought so hard to maintain. "Where the hell would I find you a husband?"

"The same place you find people to fill the positions normally. Interview. We're in New York—if *you* can't find a single man who's willing to at least consider this, then no one can."

Gideon started to tell her exactly how impossible it was, but guilt rose and choked the words off. He thought this plan was bat-shit crazy, and the thought of Lucy in some loveless marriage irritated him like sandpaper beneath his skin, scratching until he might go mad from it.

But it wasn't his call to make.

And he was partially to blame for her single status right now.

Fuck.

Gideon straightened. No matter what he thought of this plan, when it came right down to the wire, he owed Lucy. He knew that piece of shit Jeff had cheated on her, and Gideon had kept his mouth shut for a full month before he'd told her the truth. That kind of debt didn't just go away. If she was coming to him now, it was because she'd exhausted all other options, and his saying no wasn't going to deter her in the least—she'd find a different way.

Really, he had no option. It might have been two years since he'd seen Lucy Baudin, but that didn't change the fact that he considered her a friend, and he'd never leave a friend hanging out to dry when they needed him. Gideon might have questionable morals about most things, but loyalty wasn't one of them.

She needed him. He'd have found a way to help her even if he didn't owe her.

At least if he was in the midst of this madness, he'd

have some ability to keep her as safe as possible. He could protect her now like he hadn't been able to protect her from the hurt Jeff had caused.

If she was crazy for coming up with the plan in the first place, he was even crazier for agreeing to it. "I'll do it."

Lucy couldn't believe the words that had just come out of his mouth. It was too good to be true. Attempting to rope Gideon Novak into this scheme had been her Hail Mary. She was desperate and he was the only one she trusted enough to even attempt something like a search for a husband. But she hadn't thought he'd actually agree to it.

He said he'd help. Shock stole her ability to speak for a full five seconds. *Say something. You know the drill—fake it until you make it. This is just another trial. Focus.* She cleared her throat. "I'm sorry—did you just say yes?"

"Yes." He studied her face with dark eyes lined with thick lashes, which she secretly envied. Gideon had always been too attractive for Lucy's state of mind. His dark hair was always styled in what she could only call "rakish," and his strong jaw and firm mouth would have kept her up at night if he wasn't firmly in the friend zone.

At least, he used to be.

She set the thought aside because going down the rabbit hole of despair that was her relationship with Jeff Larsson was out of the question. It had ended, and her friendship with Gideon had been a casualty of war.

Until now.

Gideon shifted, bringing her back to the present. "How exactly were you planning on going about this?"

This, at least, she had an answer for. Lucy had spent entirely too much time reviewing the steps required to get to her goal with minimum fuss—a husband and her promotion. "I thought you could come up with a list of suitable candidates, I could have a date or two with each, and then we could narrow the list down from there."

"Mmm-hmm." He tapped his fingers on his knee, dragging her attention south of his face. He wore a three-piece suit, which should have been too formal for this meeting, but Gideon managed to pull it off all the same. The pin-striped gray-on-gray gave him an old-world kind of feel, like something out of *Mad Men*.

Thankfully for Lucy, he had better morals than Don Draper.

She fought not to squirm in her seat under the weight of his attention. It was easy enough to be distanced and professional when she'd laid out her proposal—she'd practiced it the same way she practiced opening and closing statements before a trial. Getting into the nitty-gritty of the actual planning and actions was something else altogether.

"I'm open to suggestions, of course." *There—look at me, being reasonable.*

"Of course." He nodded as if deciding something. "We do this, we do it on my terms. I pick the men. I supervise the dates. And if I don't like the look of any of them, I have veto rights."

Veto rights? That wasn't part of the plan. She shook her head. "No. Absolutely not."

"You came to me, Lucy. That means you trust my judgment." He gave her an intense look that made her skin feel too tight. "Those are the terms."

Terms. Damn, she'd forgotten the most important thing.

It doesn't have to be the most important thing. He doesn't know it was part of the plan, so it's not too late to back out.

But if she backed out, the deep-rooted fear from her time with her ex would never be exorcised. She'd spend the rest of her life—and her prospective marriage—second-guessing herself and her husband. It would drive her crazy and ultimately poison everything.

She couldn't let it happen, no matter how humiliating she found asking for Gideon's help with this.

Lucy managed to drag her gaze away from his. She pulled at the hem of her skirt. "There's one more thing."

"I'm listening."

She smoothed her suddenly sweating palms over her desk. "Are you seeing anyone?"

"What the hell does that have to do with anything?"

It had everything to do with things. She'd never known Gideon to hold down a relationship longer than a few weeks, but that didn't mean he hadn't somehow changed in the last two years. The entire second part of her plan leaned heavily on the assumption that he *hadn't* changed.

The Gideon she'd known before had been her friend,

yes, but he'd also been a playboy to the very definition of the word. He hadn't dated seriously. He'd never mistreated women, but he hadn't kept them around for long, either. Lucy had heard the whispers in college about his expertise in the bedroom—it was legendary enough that most women ignored the fact they had an expiration date from the moment he showed an interest in them.

To put it simply, he was *perfect* for her current situation.

She just had to find the strength to speak the damn words. She forced her hands still. "I'm going to need… lessons."

"Lucy, look at me."

Helpless, she obeyed. He frowned at her like he was trying to read her mind. "You're going to have to explain what the hell you're talking about."

It was so much harder to get it out while looking at him. She pressed her lips together. She'd faced down some of the most vicious prosecutors New York had to offer. She could damn well face Gideon Novak down, too.

You know these words. You've practiced them often enough.

"I need lessons of the sexual nature." He went so still, he might as well have turned to stone, so she charged on. "This might be an arranged marriage, so to speak, but it would be a true marriage. And, as I don't cherish the idea of being cheated on by yet another fiancé, that means sex needs to be part of the bargain. It's been a long time for me, and I have to brush up on my skill set."

Not to mention the only man I ever slept with was Jeff, and he never missed an opportunity to tell me how uninspiring he found our sex life.

Or that he blamed his cheating on my being unable to meet his needs.

She didn't let what Jeff thought dictate her life anymore, but Lucy would be lying if she pretended his words didn't haunt her—that they hadn't been instrumental in her two-year celibate streak. She'd enjoyed sex. She'd thought Jeff had enjoyed it, as well. If she could be so terribly wrong on such a fundamental level before, what was to stop her from failing at it again?

No, she couldn't allow it. If she trusted Gideon enough to secure his help finding a husband, then she trusted him enough to create a safe space to teach her something she obviously needed to know to be an effective wife. His rumored sex prowess just sweetened the bargain, because he was more than experienced enough to walk her through a crash course in seduction.

He still hadn't said anything.

She sighed. "I know it's a lot to ask—"

"I'm going to stop you right there." He stood and adjusted his jacket as he buttoned it. "I will charge you for the husband hunting—the same rates of a normal client. I'm not a sex worker, Lucy. You can't wave a magic wand and acquire lessons in fucking."

She did her best not to wilt.

You knew it was a long shot.

"I understand."

"That said…" He shook his head like he couldn't believe the words coming out of his mouth any more than she could. "Come by my place tonight. We'll talk. After that, we'll see."

That…wasn't a no. It wasn't a yes. But it most definitely wasn't a no.

"Okay." She didn't dare say anything more in fear that he'd change his mind. *I can't believe this is happening.* He didn't look happy to have offered the invitation. In fact, Gideon looked downright furious.

He pinned her with a look. "Seven. You remember the address."

It wasn't a question but she still nodded all the same. "I'll be there."

"Don't be late." He turned and stalked out of her office, leaving her staring after him.

What just happened?

A thrill coursed through her. What just happened was that Gideon Novak had agreed to help her. Professionally he had a reputation for always getting his man and, personally, he had everything required to get her pending marriage off to the right start.

He said yes.

With him in her corner, there was no way she'd fail. The promotion was hers. She could feel it.

CHAPTER TWO

GIDEON SWAM LAPS until every muscle in his body shook with exhaustion. It didn't help. All he could see was Lucy's earnest expression as those sinful lips spoke words he would have killed to hear before. *Teach me.* His attraction for that woman had never brought him anything but trouble, and apparently he was doubling down because he hadn't told her no like he damn well should have. Instead he'd told her to come to his place.

So they could talk.

About him giving her lessons in fucking.

He pulled himself out of the pool and climbed to his feet. He'd been prepared to tell her no—to both the husband hunt and the lessons. Instead he'd invited her over tonight. What the hell was that about?

You know what that's about.

Gideon wanted Lucy.

He'd wanted her from the moment he'd seen her across that crowded bar in Queens six years ago. She'd been so fresh-faced and, even too many shots in, he'd known there was something special about her.

Unfortunately so had Jeff Larsson, and that bastard had beaten him to the punch—meeting Lucy, dating Lucy, proposing to Lucy.

Gideon had tried his damnedest to be happy for his best friend—and to table his desire for his best friend's woman—but it had never quite gone away. It didn't matter how many girls he'd dated, because his heart had never been in it. When Jeff had made a passing remark on Gideon's tendency to find willowy brunettes with freckles, he'd shelved dating completely and restricted his interactions to one night.

He showered and dressed quickly. It would be tricky getting back to his place before she arrived, but he'd had to do something to take the edge off or he was in danger of throwing caution to the wind. The temptation of Lucy in his bed, even for such a shitty reason…

He'd be a bastard and a half to do it.

No, Gideon would grab takeout, sit her down to her favorite Chinese and explain all the reasons why sex between them wasn't an option. He'd be calm and reasonable and use whatever arguments he had to get his point across. She didn't need *lessons*. No man with a pulse and a working cock was going to have a problem with anything Lucy had to offer.

His step hitched at the thought of someone else waking up next to her every morning. Of the long nights buried between her thighs and the friction of sweat-slicked skin and—

Fuck.

He glanced back at the gym, seriously considering calling the whole thing off and spending the next three hours back in the pool. Maybe if he was too exhausted to move, his fury at the thought of her with another man would subside.

He knew better.

If he hadn't been happy that his best friend was with her—even before the idiot had started fucking around—he wasn't going to be pleased with a stranger. There was no help for it. Lucy would charge ahead with this plan of hers whether he agreed to it or not. He might be able to talk her out of the sex bit, but he wouldn't be able to convince her that she didn't need a husband.

He'd failed her when it came to Jeff. Even as his best friend, Gideon had missed the warning signs until it was almost too late—and then he'd hesitated a full month before breaking the news to her. He'd well and truly fucked up across the board and it had cost him her friendship—something he'd valued more than he could have dreamed.

He wouldn't fuck up again.

She wanted a husband? Well, then, Gideon was going to find her the most honorable man he could to make her happy. He owed it to her to do so.

He barely had time to drop the takeout on the kitchen counter when a knock sounded. He skirted the couch and opened the door. "You're early."

"I hope you don't mind. Your doorman remembered me, so he didn't bother to buzz you." She gave a tentative smile that pulled at him despite his determination to do the right thing.

Lucy must have made it home because she'd changed into a pair of black leggings and a lightweight slouchy shirt that seemed determined to slide off one shoulder. She saw him looking and bit her bottom lip. "I know we talked about lessons, and this isn't exactly seduction personified, but I went through my closet and, aside from work clothes, I don't think I *own* anything that's 'seduction personified.'"

For fuck's sake, she was killing him. Gideon stepped back and held the door open. "You look fine."

"Fine." She frowned. "I know you're cranky about being cornered with this whole thing, but you don't have to damn me with faint praise. I asked you to do this because I trust you to tell me the truth. I've always trusted you to tell me the truth."

If she'd taken out a knife and stabbed him in the heart, it would have stung less. Gideon closed the door carefully behind her, trying to maintain his control. It didn't matter how honest she thought he was, he wouldn't agree to take her to bed. He couldn't. "This won't work if you're going to jump down my throat every time I say something. I said you look fine. You do. I didn't tell you to dress for seduction, Lucy. I said to get your ass over here so we can talk. That—" he motioned at her clothes "—is perfectly adequate for a conversation between two friends."

"Right. Okay. I'm sorry. I'm nervous." She pulled at her shirt, which caused it to drop another inch down her arm.

Gideon had never found shoulders particularly provocative before but he wanted to drag his mouth over the line of her collarbone. *Keep it together, asshole.* He cleared his throat and looked away. "You don't need lessons, Lucy. Not from me. Not from anyone. You're beautiful and any man would be lucky to have you in his bed."

"If you don't want to teach me, that's fine. I did say that this morning." She wandered farther into his apartment and circled the couch he'd bought six months ago. It was slate gray with dark blue accents, and the saleswoman had insisted it would pull the room together in a way he'd love. He was still waiting to love it. Lucy picked up one of the ridiculous blue throw pillows and hugged it to her chest. "I'm not fishing for a compliment, by the way, but thank you. Though, beauty only goes so far. Since you haven't… We haven't…" She huffed out a breath. "Can I be perfectly frank?"

"You weren't before now?" If she was franker, she might actually kill him.

"Jeff might be a cheating bastard, but that doesn't change the fact that even before he started sleeping around, he was never…satisfied. Since he obviously found that satisfaction with those other women, it's impossible to blame the entire problem on him."

Gideon watched her pick at the tassels on the pillow while he dissected what she'd just said.

"You've been with other men since him."

"No." She still wouldn't look up. "I almost did once. But I kept hearing *his* voice in my head with those nasty little comments that he always wrote off as a joke and

I just couldn't. I know that's pathetic, but after a while, the risk of finding out that Jeff was really right all along wasn't worth the potential pleasure. So I focused on work instead of dating—and now here we are."

Gideon wished he could go back in time and deliver a few more punches to Jeff's perfect face. He'd known things weren't perfect with Jeff and Lucy, but he hadn't realized just how much of a dick his friend had been. "He's a piece of shit."

"I'm not arguing that, believe me." She gave a faint smile. "Thank you again for saving me from marrying him. I don't know if I ever said it before, but it couldn't have been easy to say something. You two had been friends for so long."

Gideon scrubbed a hand over his face. He read people for a living—both his clients and the people he found to fill the open positions. He was damn good at it, too. That skill made him the best in the business and ensured that he almost always got the secondary bonus for the position still being filled for a year after the initial contract.

Every instinct he had was insisting that Lucy's sheepish smile covered up a soul wound. If he was a good man, he'd let someone else help her heal from that—someone who'd be there for the long term. Likely that theoretical husband he was supposed to find her. But Gideon wasn't a good man.

He didn't want it to be anyone else.

He wanted it to be *him*.

"Sit down."

She dropped onto the couch, still clinging to the pillow. “Okay.”

There wasn’t a convenient playbook for how to go about this, but they *did* need to have a conversation before it went any further. “I will give you…lessons. On two conditions.”

“Agreed.”

He shot her a look. “Hear the conditions first and then decide if you’re good with them. First—you communicate with me. You like something? Tell me. You aren’t into it? You need to speak up. You fake anything and we call the whole thing off. I can’t help you if you aren’t honest with both yourself and me.”

She wrinkled her nose. “Fine. I’m an adult. I can talk about sex.”

He didn’t comment on the fact she seemed to be trying to convince herself. The confidence and ice queen bit she’d played in the office was nowhere to be seen now, which made him wonder who was the real Lucy—the cold and professional lawyer or the unsure woman sitting in front of him now.

Gideon leaned forward. “Second condition is that you’re not with anyone else for the duration.”

“Why?” She held up a hand. “I have no intention of being with anyone else, but I’m curious.”

“It’s respect.” *Liar. It’s jealousy.* He smothered the snide little voice and kept his tone even. “We’re exclusive—both of us—until the expiration date.”

“Exclusive.” She said the word as if tasting it. “When’s the expiration date?”

Never. Fuck, he was already in over his head and

sinking fast and he hadn't even touched her. "When you decide on a candidate for a husband, we end it."

Lucy nodded. "That seems reasonable. Should we start now?" She reached for her shirt.

"Holy fuck, slow down." He made an effort to lower his voice and held out a hand. "You want lessons? We start with the basics. Come here."

She reluctantly let go of the pillow and rose to cross over to his chair. Lucy eyed his hand, but ultimately placed hers in it. Gideon drew her down slowly, giving her plenty of time to see where things were going. She obliged him by climbing into his lap, though she held herself so stiffly she felt downright brittle.

He kept hold of her hand and set his other on her hip. It would have been innocent if not for the fact that she was straddling him and his cock had not gotten the memo about moving slow.

She shifted, her eyes going wide. "Ah…"

"Are you uncomfortable?" He spoke before she could think too hard.

"No…" She bit her lip. "Right. Honesty. Okay, yes, this feels weird. Awkward. I don't know where to put my hands and I can feel you, and it's making me nervous."

She was right. It was awkward as fuck. But Gideon wasn't going to throw her off the deep end on the first night, no matter how surreal this whole thing was. She trusted him to take care of her and he'd do whatever it took to be worthy of that trust. *Do whatever it took to keep her from changing her mind.* He kept his voice low so as not to startle her. "I'm going to kiss you now."

"Okay." She licked her lips and carefully tilted forward.

Gideon moved his hand from her hip to cup her jaw, guiding her down as he leaned up to brush his mouth against hers. She smelled of citrus and he had to fight to keep a growl internal. *Nice and easy.* He nipped her bottom lip and then soothed it with his tongue. She placed her hands on his biceps and relaxed against him, bit by bit. Gideon took it slow. He kissed her, keeping it light, until she shifted restlessly against him.

Then, and only then, did he slip his tongue into her mouth.

His first taste of Lucy went straight to his head. He used his hand on her jaw to angle her to allow him deeper and stroked his tongue against hers. Slow and steady was the name of the game.

Lucy whimpered and went soft against him. Her body melded to his, her breasts dragging against his chest with each inhalation. She shifted her grip and tentatively sifted her fingers through his hair. As if she wasn't sure of her welcome.

He wanted her sure.

Gideon shifted back to lean against the chair. The move settled her tighter against him as her knees sank into the cushion on either side of his hips. She gasped into his mouth and he ate the sound. He kissed her like he'd wanted to since that first night, when he'd heard her infectious laugh across a crowded bar. She tasted just as sunny as she smelled, as addicting as a summer's day in the midst of winter.

He couldn't get enough.

CHAPTER THREE

LUCY'S AWKWARDNESS WENT up in smoke the second Gideon kissed her. She'd expected... Well, she wasn't sure what she'd expected. For him to take her into the bedroom and strip them down and just go for it. Preferably with the lights turned off to hide her mortification.

He stroked his hands up the sides of her face and tangled his fingers in her hair. The move pulled her out of their kiss, but Gideon didn't let the distance stand. He dragged his mouth down the line of her neck, raising goose bumps in his wake.

A deep, hidden ember inside her burst into flame.

She was doing this. She was straddling Gideon Novak with his mouth on her skin and his hands on her body. Something she'd never even allowed herself to *think* about until she'd come up with this plan.

"You're thinking too hard."

"I can't believe this is happening."

He set his teeth against her collarbone. "If you change your mind—"

"I won't." She'd never dared fantasize about him—

she hadn't let herself cross that line, even in her mind—but she wasn't missing this opportunity for the world. Warmth flared with each breath, the heat centered at her core, where she could feel his cock lining up right where she wanted it.

I want it.

The realization startled her, though it shouldn't have. Gideon was sex personified and having all his considerable attention focused solely on her was a heady feeling. She wanted… More. All of it. Everything he could give her. She moaned. "More."

Gideon took her mouth. There was no other way to put it. He claimed her, establishing dominance with a stroke of his tongue, engulfing her entire world in that single contact. He tasted like peppermint—a shocking sensation against her tongue. Unexpected.

Just like the man himself.

It wasn't enough. There were too many clothes between them. She could feel his broad shoulders flexing, could test the definition of his muscles as she slid her hands down his chest, but his button-up shirt barred her from the skin-to-skin contact she craved.

Her breasts felt too tight, her nipples pebbling until they almost hurt. At least her yoga pants didn't offer much in the way of a barrier as she rocked her hips against him. His slacks did little to hide the size of his cock, and that little movement felt deliciously good. Intoxicating. So she did it again.

Gideon dropped one hand to her hip. For one horrifying moment she thought he'd stop her—maybe tell her that grown adults did not dry hump in the middle of one's living room—but he just urged her on. He never stopped kissing her, never stopped exploring her mouth. As if kissing was his be-all and end-all rather than just the first step to get to sex.

God, I am so messed up.

He squeezed her ass and nipped her bottom lip. "How we doing?"

"Good." Was that her voice? She sounded like she was doing something requiring a whole lot more exertion than kissing Gideon Novak. *If this is what* kissing *is like, am I going to survive actual sex?*

Who cares? It'd be a glorious way to go.

He used his grip on her hip to pull her closer yet, lining up his cock with her clit. "And now?"

She hissed out a breath. *Please don't stop.* She could come like this if they kept it up. "Really good. But—" She didn't want to talk about it, didn't want to do anything to make this stop, so she went in for another kiss.

Gideon tightened his hold on her hair just enough to prevent her from moving. "But?"

His insistence on honesty had seemed like a good idea at the time—how could she improve if she didn't know what she was doing wrong?—but in practice it felt like he was stripping her bare in a way that had nothing to do with sex. She closed her eyes, because it was easier to answer when she wasn't meeting his gaze. "Isn't dry humping kind of juvenile?" *Are you going to mock me if I orgasm from this? Maybe make a joke about cobwebs or how long it's been for me?*

His chuckle pulled at things low in her stomach. "Does this feel juvenile to you?"

"No." It felt hotter than it should have and even a little dirty. She wanted it too much, and that was the problem. She forced herself to open her eyes and found him watching her with a contemplative expression. "What?"

"Pleasure isn't something you can put limits on, Lucy. There isn't a right way to go about it. Would you tell someone who was eating one of those double-chocolate-death desserts you love so much that they were eating it wrong if they did it differently than you?"

"Of course not." She blinked. How had he possibly remembered her favorite dessert?

"Then why is *this* wrong?" He urged her to rock against him again. "Feels good to me. Feels good to you. No reason to overthink it."

When Gideon put it like that, it sounded so simple. Deceptively simple. She started to ask another question but forced herself to silence it. This insecurity wasn't her. This was the ghost of her relationship with Jeff coloring the current interaction.

Exactly what she'd been afraid would happen.

"Thank you for agreeing to this, Gideon. You didn't have to and—"

"Lucy." He framed her face with his big hands, preventing her from looking away. Those dark eyes were so incredibly serious. "Stop thanking me for this. The matchmaking shit? Sure. Not this. You're crazy if you think I'm not getting something out of it—same as you. Enjoy it. Enjoy *me*. It's as simple as that."

Easier said than done. The malicious voice that had spent far too many years lurking in the back of her mind wouldn't be silenced. Not completely. *Pity fuck.* She pressed her lips together. "I want to have sex now."

"No."

She frowned. "What?"

"No." He sat up, forcing her to grab his shoulders to stabilize herself, and then stood, taking her with him. "You want me to teach you? Then we're doing this on my terms. You were enjoying the hell out of this and something tripped you up." He laid them down on his ridiculously comfortable couch. She sank into the cushions as his weight settled over her. It felt good. Right.

It scared the shit out of her.

"Gideon."

"My terms, Lucy." He kissed her again. Before it had been sweet, and then intense, but she hadn't realized he was holding back until that moment. Gideon kissed her like he owned her. He took her mouth, urging her to meet him halfway.

She held back for all of one second; it was impossible to maintain distance with his very presence overwhelming her. So she let go, tangling her tongue with his. The second she did, he started to move.

It had felt good when she was on top, but it was nothing compared to him pressing her into the couch as he stroked his cock against her clit. One long slide up and then another back down. The desire that had been put on hold while she'd let her insecurities get the best of her seared her—with interest. As if it'd been waiting for her to just let go and enjoy this moment for what it was. *Pleasure. No questions asked.*

She arched up to meet him. "That feels good."

Gideon hitched a hand beneath her knee and drew her leg up and out, opening her farther. He kissed her again and kept up that slow drag that had sparks dancing at her nerve endings. Her body wound tighter and tighter with each stroke until she teetered on the brink. Lucy writhed against him, trying to get closer, to get him where she needed him, to do whatever it took to reach that edge. "Gideon, *please*."

He shifted back and she sobbed out a breath at the loss of him. But he didn't make her wait long. He slid a hand beneath the waistband of her yoga pants and into her panties. His rough curse would have made her smile under other circumstances, but she was too busy holding her breath. *So close. Please just touch me.*

He did.

He made a V with his fingers and slid it over her clit in the exact same motion he'd been doing with his cock before. She lasted three strokes before she came apart in his arms, her pleasure drawing a cry from her lips and blanking out her mind into delicious static. He softened their kiss to the barest brushing of lips and then shifted to the side so his weight wasn't completely on her.

Lucy blinked at the pale gray ceiling and tried to reconcile what had just happened with reality. *I just came. Without pressure. Without having to force it or fake it.* A world-ending orgasm and *Gideon* was the one who'd coaxed it from her. "Wow." As soon as the word popped out of her mouth, she cringed. *What a stupid thing to say.* She was hardly a virgin and she wasn't an idiot teenager, no matter what they'd just done.

Gideon gave another of those low laughs. "All flavors, Lucy."

Against her better judgment, she couldn't help comparing what they'd just done to her experiences with Jeff when they'd first started dating. Night and day. Even though it'd taken her and Jeff a bit to work up to sex, he'd always had an air of impatience about him when they were intimate—like he couldn't wait to get to the next step. Add that to his competitive need to make her come multiple times every time they were together and the pressure had twisted with the desire until it made her jumpy every time they'd been alone together. Things had changed a little once they'd finally had sex, but then other elements had come into play.

Boring.

Uninspired.

Like fucking a doll.

"Lucy, look at me." Gideon's voice drew her out of the horror show that was her past.

She shook her head. *God, I can't even do this right.* What they'd just done was so incredibly perfect and she'd had to go and ruin it by letting her issues with her ex creep in. "I'm sorry."

"No, I'm sorry." He stroked a hand through her hair, the move so tender, her stomach tried to tie itself in knots. His dark eyes took on a distance as he looked at something she couldn't see. "I knew Jeff was an asshole, but if I'd known what a piece of shit he was, I would have warned you off before he got his hooks into you."

"It wouldn't have mattered." Six years ago, in the midst of her headlong rush into adulthood, she was so sure that she knew better, she hadn't listened to anyone. Not her sister, not her friends, not her fledgling instincts. As nice as it was to think otherwise, she wouldn't have listened to Gideon, either.

Being this close to him, talking like this while her body still sang from the pleasure he'd given her… It was too intimate. Too revealing. Just plain too much.

She slid off the couch and stood. A quick look at the front of his slacks confirmed that he was still, in fact, painfully hard. *Nice job, Lucy. Bask in your post-orgasmic bliss and ignore the fact he's still in need.* "Do you want me to…?"

"These lessons aren't about me." He sat up. "They're about you. And you need space."

Yeah, she did. His airy living room was suddenly too small, the walls closing in even as her heart beat too fast. "I asked for this."

"You don't have to explain." He gave her a half smile that didn't reach his eyes. "We poked at some old wounds tonight. If that means you need some distance from the whole thing, then so be it. You're being honest, and fuck if I'm going to punish you for that." He grabbed his phone off the coffee table. "But if you're headed home, I'm calling you a cab."

She should push back. She was more than capable of calling her own damn cab and the subway would be running for hours yet. But if Gideon could respect her need to flee without his pride being injured and throwing a fit, she could respect his need to get her home safe. “Okay.”

He made the call quickly and set the phone down. “What’s your schedule look like tomorrow?”

The change in subject left her discombobulated. “I have court in the afternoon, so I’ll be doing last-minute preparations beforehand.” It was as close to an open-and-shut case as such things got. The cops had mishandled the evidence and the lead detective had an established vendetta against her client. She had every intention of getting the whole damn thing thrown out.

“I know that look on your face. You have this one in the bag.”

Her stomach gave another of those flutters that wasn’t altogether uncomfortable. He’d said that with such confidence, as if there wasn’t a single doubt in his mind that she would win. Lucy tucked a strand of hair behind her ear. “I should be free in the evening.” *For another lesson?* She didn’t know if she’d look forward to it or dread it. *Liar. You haven’t even left yet and you’re already craving another hit.*

“Good.” He stood, suddenly taking up too much space. She tensed, half expecting him to touch her. But Gideon headed for the door. “I’ll have a list of preliminary candidates ready for you, and we’ll go over them at dinner.”

“That I’ll pay for.” She cast a pointed look at the way his jaw tensed at her words. “Don’t be like that. If I was a normal client, I’d pay and you wouldn’t blink because that’s how things are done.”

"You aren't a normal client, Lucy. There's nothing *normal* about this." He motioned between them.

She couldn't really argue that, but that didn't mean he'd win this battle. "I'll handle the reservations and text you the details."

"Stubborn."

The twisting in her stomach took on a sour edge. Jeff had thrown that word at her like a curse more often than she could count. *Stop it. Oh, my God,* stop. *He's in the past and he's staying there.* "It's my best trait."

"I wouldn't dream of arguing that." He held the door open for her. "Until tomorrow."

"See you then."

She headed for the elevator, stopping several steps down the hallway and leaning against the wall as she tried to calm her racing heart. She hadn't known it could be like this. He'd just…taken care of her. Both physically and emotionally. Bringing her to orgasm and recognizing and respecting the panic driving her to leave. Lucy hadn't expected that. She didn't know what to do with a version of Gideon who was different than she'd expected.

What did I get myself into?

CHAPTER FOUR

"YOU'RE FUCKING CRAZY."

Gideon didn't look up from his computer. "You don't have to tell me that."

"And yet I'm telling you all the same. What the hell are you doing? *Matchmaker?* For *Lucy Baudin*?" Roman Bassani paced from one side of the room to the other, his restless energy irritating as fuck.

"I know we're supposed to have lunch, but this came up and can't wait. I'm going to have to take a rain check." Gideon wrote down another name and moved to the next candidate on his preliminary list. When Roman paced another lap around the office, he cursed. "Sit down or get out. You're distracting me."

"You need the distraction. Hell, you need a goddamn intervention." Roman threw himself into the chair across from the desk and slouched. He would have been at home in some artsy perfume ad with his brooding good looks and the way he seemed to pose without noticing he was doing it. On any other man, the affected attitude would have pissed Gideon off, but with Roman it was just… Roman. He was too honest, too brash, too comfortable in any space. It was part of what made him so good at his job—he had never met a challenge he wasn't fully confident he could tackle.

Whether his confidence was misplaced or not was an argument for another day.

"Gideon, why are you doing this? Wait—don't tell me. You're not still feeling guilty because you didn't tell her what a douche Jeff was immediately? Look, we all fucked up. You're the only one who stepped in, and that's something I have to live with." He made a face. "I convinced myself that it wasn't my place or my business."

"Jeff's good at spinning any situation to benefit him." He'd sure as hell laid on the guilt and idiotic bro code heavy enough to give even Gideon pause at the time.

"Changes nothing." Roman shrugged. "Including the fact that you are not qualified to be a matchmaker, let alone for Lucy. She's a good girl and, damn it, she deserves a professional. I know a few in the city. I can call in a favor and get her shoved to the top of the list and wrap this whole thing up without anyone crossing any lines."

He tried to be rational and actually consider it. He fucking failed. The line had been crossed last night and there was no going back now. "No. She asked me, so I'm the one who'll do it. And don't get any funny ideas, Roman. You meddle in enough people's lives. I have no interest in being added to the list."

"As if you'd let me." Roman affected a sigh. "You're as mean as a junkyard dog."

"And you're wasting my time. Unless you have something worthwhile to add to the search, get out."

He realized his mistake the second his friend perked up. "Who's on the list?"

Fuck me. "No."

"Come on." Roman shot to his feet, towering over the desk, and snatched the paper from beneath Gideon's hand. His hazel eyes went wide. "Shit, Gideon. You put Aaron Livingston on here. Shooting for the stars, aren't you?"

"She's worth it." He grabbed the paper.

Roman studied him for a long moment. "Interesting."

"For fuck's sake, Roman, don't you have some business to buy up or small children to terrify?" He still had several hours' worth of work to do before he met up with Lucy tonight. The address she'd texted him wasn't far, but rush hour would be a bitch to navigate, so he'd scheduled in extra time. That didn't mean he was going to dick around with this damn list.

His friend pointed to two names on the list. "Take Travis and David off the list. They're fuckheads with women, though they both hide it well."

Gideon crossed out their names. "I hadn't heard."

"Why would you? You don't date, and that handsome mug of yours might have people intrigued, but it's from a distance. People aren't rushing to confide in you because there's a solid chance you'll rip them a new one for wasting your time."

Gideon glared. "Are you finished?"

"Not yet." Roman gave a lazy grin. "My point is that people talk to me, so using that as a resource is a smart thing to do. Aaron Livingston is as straight as they come. If that guy has any skeletons in his closet, they're buried deep. The other two left on the list are up in the air. I'll find out what I can and let you know."

He fought down the need to snap back. The truth was that Roman was right. People didn't open up to Gideon. His clients only cared that he got the job done and had one of the highest ratings in the industry. The people he placed for his clients only cared about their endgame in a company that would pay them well to do what they loved. Friends? He had them. He just preferred them at a distance.

Roman had never been able to take that hint.

"Fine. Look into them."

"It's charming that you think I need your permission." Roman grinned. "I'll come by in the next few days and let you know what I dig up."

A call would have been preferable, but Gideon knew Roman well enough to know that arguing was pointless. His friend did what he wanted, when he wanted. He sighed. "Fine."

"Chin up, Novak." Roman paused. "All joking aside, if you're going to do this, do it right. I know your history with Lucy is complicated, but playing this straight is the only way. Otherwise, there are a lot of potential complications that could arise."

Last night had been nothing if not one long, agonizingly good complication. Even almost twenty-four hours later, he could still taste her in his mouth. It made him crave more, which was a dangerous path to walk.

Lucy wasn't for him.

He had to remember that.

If she'd wanted *him*, she would have said so. Even this almost-timid version of her wouldn't have balked at putting it out there. She was direct, as evidenced by her plan existing in the first place. But she hadn't brought him into her office to ask *him* to step into the role of husband.

Husband.

What would that even look like?

Gideon shook his head and focused on his friend. "I have it under control."

"Keep telling yourself that." Roman headed for the door. "I'll check in tomorrow, but in case I don't see you before then, we still on for Friday?"

"Yeah." They had a standing reservation in Vortex's VIP lounge on Friday nights. It was one of the only social appointments he held consistently, despite occasionally running into Jeff there. But that asshole had started coming less and less in the years since he and Lucy had broken off their engagement. People had started to see through his charming act and called him out when he was acting like a douchebag—which was often.

"See you then." Roman opened the door and paused. "You should bring her."

Gideon tore his gaze away from the list of names yet again. “What?”

“You should bring Lucy on Friday. I know Aaron Livingston since we worked together last year. We can orchestrate a non-pressure meeting. You’re on your own with the other two, but I don’t think Aaron would agree to a blind date for shits and giggles.”

Since Gideon had only met him in passing, he couldn’t argue that. “Do it.” He spoke before he had a chance to think up half a dozen reasons why it was a bad idea. It *wasn’t* a bad idea. It was his issue if he didn’t want to see her with someone else—not hers.

He waited for Roman to shut the door behind him before he grabbed his phone. Both Mark and Liam were acquaintances he’d come across in the last few years who had seemed like upstanding guys. He’d feel them out for interest and then take the list to Lucy to see where she stood with all of it.

The knowledge that she’d likely end up with one of these men sat in his stomach like a rock. He hesitated, his contact list staring back at him. It would be the easiest thing in the world to sabotage this. All he had to do was feed some false information about Lucy and they’d say no. Or feed her false information about *them* to prove New York had a shitty dating scene.

“No.” He’d promised her to do his best and he’d damn well do his best. Gideon had lied to her once before and it had almost destroyed them both. He wasn’t going to do that to her again.

Fuck, he was in this situation *because* of what happened before.

Gideon would do right by Lucy. He'd have to be a heartless bastard to do anything else. The only option was to find her a damn husband.

No matter what it cost him to do it.

Lucy was on her second glass of wine by the time she caught sight of Gideon's familiar form moving toward her table through the darkened room. He towered over the tiny host and the poor man kept shooting looks over his shoulder as if he expected Gideon to club him over the head. The thought made her smile and was almost enough to distract her from her nervousness.

She'd woken up this morning from the single hottest dream of her life, starring none other than Gideon Novak. It started identical to their encounter last night, but they hadn't stopped until they were naked and in his bed, both shaking from their respective orgasms. Her body flushed at the memory and she took a shaky sip of wine.

What was the protocol for greeting a man who'd used his fingers to make her come on his couch the night before? They weren't dating, so a kiss seemed inappropriate. They weren't even really friends anymore, so a hug was likely presumptuous. A handshake was just absurd.

Gideon saved her from having to decide by sitting before she had a chance to stand. He shot a look at the host. He probably meant it as a polite dismissal, but it actually looked scathing. Lucy watched the man nearly run from the table. "You really have to work on your attitude."

"My attitude is fine."

"Without a doubt, but you have a very intimidating persona. You know most women judge a man by how he treats the waitstaff on their first date—and you would have just nixed the possibility of a second date and we haven't even had appetizers yet."

Gideon raised his eyebrows. "Good day in court, I take it."

"We're not talking about me." She leaned forward and lowered her voice. Enjoying poking at him a little. "Though that was a very smooth change of subject."

The corners of his lips twitched upward. "Yes, it was. We're not here to talk about my dating prospects. We're here to talk about yours." He looked up as a waiter approached and she actually saw the effort he put into forcing a smile. It looked downright pained, but it was better than nothing. "I'll have a seven and seven." He glanced at her half-full wineglass. "Another?"

"Sure." She didn't drink more than two glasses often, but she'd busted her ass on today's case and the judge had been persuaded to dismiss the entire thing. It was a coup that should have been the tipping point for her promotion, but when Rick Parker had come by her office to congratulate her, he'd made a comment about the big, broody man who'd been in to see her yesterday. Because, of course, who she was or wasn't dating was just as important as her professional skill set.

Well, damn it, Parker's crappy attitude wasn't going to ruin her night.

"Tell me about the case."

She almost refocused the conversation, but the truth was that she didn't have anyone to talk to about it. Her sister was supportive and wonderful, but Becka had her own thing going on and couldn't be less interested in law. Get together for drinks and chat about life and what their parents were up to? Sure. Hash out the details of whatever case Lucy was working on? Not a chance. And Gideon actually looked interested.

She picked up her wineglass. "I got the entire case thrown out today. All they had was circumstantial evidence and a bad attitude about my guy's priors. They were so certain he did the crime, they didn't look at anyone else. Anyone on the outside would have come to the same conclusion, but it's always a crapshoot with Judge Jones."

"That's great, Lucy. Congrats."

"Thanks." She smiled and then took a drink. "How was your day?"

"Productive." He leaned over and pulled a tablet out of his briefcase. "I have some things to show you."

Disappointment coated her tongue when he slid the tablet across the table to her. They'd barely gotten their conversation started and now they were back to business. *You hired him as a business decision. You don't get to have it both ways.* It wasn't fair to ask him to go back to being her friend along with her being his client.

She picked up the tablet and found pictures of three men. She clicked on the first one—a blond guy with a close-cropped beard and a seriously expensive suit—and found a file. "'Aaron Livingston, born May thirteenth…'" He'd compiled a list of information ranging from where Aaron was born to where he graduated high school and college—and his GPA at both. There was also a notification about possible likes and dislikes. "Wow, Gideon. You really don't do anything halfway, do you?"

He had compiled the same information for each of the other two men. Interestingly enough, all three of them were local and had gone to prestigious business colleges, graduating close to the top of their class. All three had moved on to respected companies and seemed to be doing well for themselves.

Using their information and ignoring their pictures, she wouldn't have been able to pick any of them out of a lineup. "This… Wow."

"You said that already." He frowned. "Is something wrong? I assumed that you were looking for someone in the same financial class as you, and leaning toward white-collar businessmen. That *is* why you came to me, correct?"

Yes, at least in theory. In reality, this whole thing was playing out much differently than she'd expected. It didn't make a bit of sense, especially because it was proceeding *exactly* how she'd hoped. "No, it's fine. They're excellent candidates."

Seeing them laid out like this, the situation just became so much more real. In a very short period of time she'd be sitting across the table from one of these men, rather than Gideon. She'd be torturing herself with wondering if they'd kiss her after dinner—if maybe they'd expect more to happen.

I'm not ready.

She took a gulp of her wine. "Can we get dinner to go?"

CHAPTER FIVE

NERVES STOLE LUCY'S voice as she and Gideon walked to her apartment. She'd intentionally picked a restaurant close to her place so that they wouldn't have to worry about a cab ride to get from point A to point B. She nodded at the doorman as he held open the door for them and then she strode to the elevator and pushed the button.

Gideon followed her inside and leaned against the elevator wall. The food in the paper bag smelled divine, but her craving was solely for the man holding it. She clasped her hands together to keep from touching him. "I want to progress tonight."

He raised his eyebrows. "I'm listening."

Why was it so challenging to say these things aloud? She was an adult. She should be able to express her needs honestly without fear of being laughed out of the building—or rejected. Lucy fisted her hands and raised her chin. The mirrors in the elevator walls and door reflected a version of her that looked ready to go several rounds on the courthouse floor. "I don't want to wait anymore. I want everything."

That predatory stillness rolled over him and his eyes seemed to flare with barely banked heat. "Bite-size steps are the smart option."

"Nothing about *this* is smart, and I think we both know that." Last night had made her skittish in a way she hadn't expected, and if she was shrewder and less stubborn, she would have called the whole thing off as a result. Instead she was pushing them toward something neither could take back.

The elevator door opened and she wasted no time walking into the hall and down to her door. There were only four apartments on this floor, each occupying their respective corner of the building. Hers faced southeast, so she often woke to the early morning sunlight streaming through her windows. At least on the days she wasn't up before dawn.

She unlocked the door and held it open for Gideon. He stopped just inside the entranceway, barely leaving room for her to slide inside behind him. She tried to see the place through his eyes. The open floor plan showcased the big floor-to-ceiling windows. The kitchen lay just to the right of the front hall, the white cabinets set off with little turquoise handles she'd found online. The living room contained a decent-size TV that she rarely used and two short couches arranged in a loose V. Her cat, Garfunkel, lifted his head and gave Gideon a death stare.

Gideon moved to the kitchen counter—white marble shot through with pale gray—and set the bag of food on it. He turned and crossed his arms over his chest. "Why the change of pace?"

"Maybe I just want you." It was the truth, but not the full truth.

He shook his head. "Honesty, Lucy."

Why had she agreed to that particular term? She pulled at the hem of her fitted blue dress. "I'm nervous. Last night was good, but I didn't expect that level of reaction, and I'm afraid if we don't get it over with, I'm going to change my mind."

"Get it over with," Gideon murmured. "Sex isn't something you 'get over with.' If you think of it that way, there's a problem somewhere."

A problem he was determined to fix if the expression on his face was anything to go by. She sliced her hand through the air. "No problem. That's not what I meant at all. My issue is that the anticipation, the will-we-or-won't-we, is driving me nuts. I want to rip it off right now—like a Band-Aid."

He stared at her for a long moment and then burst out laughing. "A Band-Aid. Fuck, woman, you really are going to kill me." He ran a hand over his face. "The anticipation is meant to be enjoyed."

She could think of a lot of words to describe how she felt standing in her apartment with Gideon and knowing they were alone and could do what they wanted for hours. *Enjoyment* didn't top the list. Her body was too hot, her lungs too tight, her core aching from need. But she knew that look on his face. If she didn't do something rash, he was going to put the brakes on and sit her down and coax her to talk through it. For someone with such a ruthless reputation, Gideon was overwhelmingly careful with her.

She knew why—he had residual guilt over not telling her immediately about Jeff's cheating ways. But she didn't care about any of that right now.

All she cared about was getting through this interaction so she could go back to breathing normally again.

Before she could talk herself out of it, Lucy unzipped the side of her dress and slid it off. She didn't look at him as she kicked the silky fabric to the side. If she thought too hard about the fact that she stood in front of him in only a pair of nude-lace panties, she might die on the spot.

A second passed. Another.

Still, he didn't say anything.

What is he doing?

Probably looking for a way to gracefully exit that wouldn't have her throwing herself from the nearest window. *Stop that right now.* She was stronger than this. Lucy looked good. She ate relatively well and hit the gym at least three times a week. Last night Gideon's physical reaction had proved that he'd wanted her. He might not have taken his release, but he wasn't remotely unaffected.

So why was he standing there without saying a word?

Stop waiting for him to make the first move.

Do it yourself.

Gathering her courage, she lifted her head and looked at him. Her first step took more effort than she could have dreamed, and the intense look on his face didn't help her any. He held himself perfectly still, every muscle coiled. Though, for the life of her, she couldn't tell if it was to keep from jumping her or to stop himself from fleeing.

Only one way to find out.

She took the last few steps that brought her close enough to touch. Tentatively she reached out and laid her hands on his chest. *Why isn't he saying anything?* She waited another few seconds but the only sound in her kitchen was the soft rush of their quickened breathing.

Maybe she'd misjudged the situation. *Oh, God, what did I do?* "If you've changed your mind, just tell me. We can pretend this whole thing never happened."

Gideon couldn't look away from Lucy. She was fucking perfect. He'd known that, of course, but seeing it without clothes barring his vision was something else altogether. Her breasts were small and high, capped with dark rose nipples. He forced himself not to reach for her as she stroked her hands down his chest and back up again.

"Gideon?"

She'd asked a question, hadn't she?

"What?" His gaze snagged on her narrow waist and the nude-lace panties that were so sheer, he could see a shadow of her slit beneath them. He cleared his throat and jerked his attention back to her face.

She frowned a little. "Did you change your mind?"

"No." He finally allowed himself to move, reaching up and covering her hands with his. "Fuck me, but you can't expect a man to be faced with the sight of you naked and still be able to hold down a conversation."

"That's sweet."

But she thought he was lying. He could read it all over her face.

It struck Gideon that he'd been playing this wrong. He'd known Jeff had hurt Lucy with his actions, and then she'd told him that she hadn't been with anyone since, and he'd gone straight to treating her like an innocent virgin. She was innocent in some ways, but by being so careful with her, he'd created room for her to doubt herself—and him.

Fuck that.

He guided her hands to his shoulders and then started unbuttoning his shirt. "You don't believe the words, and I don't blame you for that. But if you won't listen to me when I tell you that you're a fucking goddess personified, then I'll show you."

She kneaded his shoulders slightly, her eyes glued to his hands as he finished with his shirt and started on the front of his slacks. "I believe you."

"You don't." He kicked off his shoes and shoved down his pants. Lucy shook her head as if fighting off a daze and pushed his shirt off his shoulders. He let it fall to the floor and then the only barriers were their respective underwear. He snagged the lace with a single finger. "These have to go."

"Yours, too."

He took a step back and hooked his thumbs in his boxer briefs. A single, smooth movement and he stood before her naked. Watching Lucy's jaw drop was ridiculously gratifying. She took in each part of his body, starting with his head and moving over his neck, his shoulders, his chest, his stomach and, finally, settling on his cock. He grew harder in response to her hungry expression.

Gideon had never had a woman look at him the way Lucy did. As if he was a present she'd found under the Christmas tree—just for her. It threatened to turn this interaction into something it could never be, so he smothered the thought. She wanted him physically. End of story.

"Gideon, you're beautiful." She shucked off her panties, never taking her gaze from him. "I mean, I'd seen you in a swimsuit, but this is different." She closed the distance between them once more, a small line appearing between her brows. "Is it weird, though? I never considered you a brother or anything like that, but you were family."

Family.

He'd forced himself to forget that feeling of belonging that Lucy seemed to extend wherever she went. When he'd hung out with her and Jeff, he'd never felt like a third wheel—he'd just been part of the unit. Of all the things he'd missed when she'd cut off communication between them, that might be the highest on the list. "I never saw you as a sister."

"I know." She laughed softly. "I'd catch you watching me sometimes—not often—and you never made it weird. But… I know."

He thought he'd hid it better than that. Gideon shoved the past away just like he shoved aside so many inconvenient feelings that seemed to arise the more time he spent with Lucy. "It's not weird."

"I guess it's not." She carefully slid her hands up his chest and around his neck, taking that last step to bring them chest to chest. He rested his hands on her waist, but she felt too good to limit the contact. Gideon stroked up her back and down again to cup her ass.

There was nothing left to say. They'd reached the point of no return the second Lucy's dress had hit the floor. Gideon lifted his head. "Bedroom."

"This way— *Oh!*"

He swept her into his arms and strode across the living room to the door she'd indicated. Her bedroom was purely Lucy: a pretty wood headboard, more pillows than one woman should require, and a bright yellow floral bedspread that brightened the room even in the low light of the single lamp she must have left on.

He laid her on the bed and settled between her thighs. Gideon had every intention of slowing things down and having a very specific conversation about how this would proceed.

Every. Intention.

But Lucy wrapped her legs around his waist and arched up to meet him, and that honorable plan disappeared as if it'd never existed. Maybe it hadn't and he'd just been lying to himself all along. It didn't matter. There was only her soft skin beneath his palms, her body sliding against his and her mouth on his neck.

He kissed her. Gideon might never get enough of her sunny taste, and he wasn't about to miss a chance to immerse himself in the feel of her. This was happening. They would cross the line he'd never once considered anything other than insurmountable.

He stroked a hand down her waist to squeeze her ass and hitch her up to fit tighter against him. The temptation to sink into her was almost too much, but this wasn't about him, his wants, his needs.

This was about Lucy.

Gideon hadn't leashed himself and his desire for her this long to skip over for anything less than the full experience. He didn't want to miss a single thing. He kissed down and across her collarbone and palmed her breasts. "Perfect. Every single thing about you is fucking perfect."

She laughed a little nervously. "You said that before."

"I'll say it again." He tongued one nipple. "Pretty and pink and…fuck. Just fucking perfect."

"Don't stop." She laced her fingers through his hair and drew him back down. "Harder."

He set his teeth gently against her nipple and then increased the pressure slightly when she went wild beneath him. Through it all, he kept his eyes open. Gideon wanted it all, every nuance of expression, every reaction. All of it.

A flush stole across her freckled cheeks and over her chest, and her small breasts heaved with each sobbed breath. He moved to give her other nipple the same treatment but kept stroking the first, pinching it with the same amount of pressure he'd applied with his mouth.

She shuddered against him, her hips grinding. "Gideon. Oh, God. I think I could come from this alone."

"I'm not done yet." He pressed one last kiss to each

nipple and then slid back until he knelt on the floor next to the bed. He grabbed her hips and jerked her to the edge. This close, he could see every part of her. Gideon drew his thumb over her slit. "You need more."

"Yes."

He used his thumbs to part her. "Next time, you'll tell me exactly what you want."

"Next time?" She lifted her head to give him a dazed look. "Why next time?"

"Because I'm a selfish bastard." His mouth actually watered being this close to the most private part of Lucy. Her pussy was as flushed as the rest of her skin, wet and wanting and practically begging for his tongue. There wasn't a single damn reason *not* to give her exactly what he wanted. "I hope you're ready."

CHAPTER SIX

LUCY HAD NEVER enjoyed oral. Not really. It was yet another area where Jeff's competitiveness soured any inkling of pleasure she might get from the act. He had a series of moves he'd go through, the goal being to get her wet enough for sex. Truth be told, she'd always suspected he didn't like the act any more than she did, but the one time she'd brought it up, it had been one of the worst fights they'd ever had.

The first rasp of whiskers against Lucy's inner thigh drove thoughts of her ex right out of her head. Gideon didn't immediately go for her clit. Instead he dragged his cheek against her other thigh, using the motion to spread her legs farther.

She lifted her head just as he dipped down and drew his tongue over her in one long lick. Then he did it again—as if she was his favorite flavor of ice cream. Considering their frenzied making out, she'd expected this to be just as quick…

Should have known better than to make assumptions about Gideon.

Especially after last time.

He spread her folds and thrust his tongue into her, his low growl making the act unbearably erotic. Lucy's thoughts slammed to a halt and her mind went gloriously blank. "Holy shit."

He didn't appear to hear her. Gideon fucked her pussy with his tongue as if he couldn't get enough of her taste. He gripped her thighs with his big hands, holding her open to his ministrations even when her muscles shook with the effort to react, to move, to do *something.*

She thrashed her head from one side to the other, the sensations too much and not enough—and she didn't know how to put it into words. *Honesty.* Words crowded in her throat, too raw and vulnerable to give voice, but then she felt his teeth and they burst forth in a rush. "My clit. Gideon, suck on my clit. Use your teeth." Like he had with her nipples. Like he was doing right now with her labia.

Her entire body coiled at the thought, and the feeling intensified when he did exactly as she asked. There was no macho posturing or telling her that he was more than capable of pleasing her without an instruction manual. Gideon just…listened.

He sucked her clit into his mouth and set his teeth against the sensitive bundle of nerve endings. She arched almost completely off the bed, and he used the move to slide his hands under her ass and lift her so he could feast more effectively.

Because that was exactly what he was doing—feasting.

There was nothing gentle or teasing about his touch

now. He went after her clit in a way that was just shy of pain, sending little zings of pure bliss through her. Her body coiled tighter yet, so close to the edge, she didn't know how much longer she could hold out.

Gideon lifted his head just enough to speak, his lips brushing her heated flesh with every word. "Do you want to come like this?"

Asking that question was the single sexiest thing anyone had ever done to her. Choice. Control. Who knew it could be such a turn-on?

She almost said yes. Lucy was so close to orgasm, she shook with need and had to focus entirely too hard to create verbal words beyond *yesyesyesyesyes*. Did she want him to keep doing what he'd been doing? Hell, yes.

But she wanted him inside her more.

She licked her lips. "I want..." How did she want him?

Every way.

Right now, though? "I want to ride you."

A muscle in his jaw ticked and his grip on her thighs twitched. "You have condoms."

"Yes." She pointed a shaking finger at her nightstand.

The ones she'd bought after her breakup had expired ages ago, victim of her self-esteem issues, so she'd picked up a new box this morning. She'd also unwrapped the box so they could save time. It had felt presumptuous in the extreme when she'd been sitting alone on her bed, Garfunkel staring at her in feline judgment. Now she wished she'd already had one of them on Gideon.

He slowly released her, as if it pained him to move away. She sat up and scooted back so she could watch him pull open the top drawer. It wasn't until his dark eyes flashed that she remembered what *else* was in the drawer. "Ah..."

He held up her pink vibrator. "We'll talk about this later." He dropped it back in the drawer and pulled out a condom. "Scratch that. We're not going to talk. I'm going to stroke myself while I watch you use it."

Her eyes went wide at the image his words painted. Him, sitting against the headboard with his cock in his hand. Her on her back with her legs spread, using her toy. Her core clenched. "I want that. Later."

"Later," he agreed. He ripped the wrapper open and proceeded to roll the condom down his length.

She stood and pushed him to sit on the edge of the bed. "Like this." Lucy climbed into his lap and reached between them to notch his cock at her entrance. With her desire driving her, it was easy to speak things that would have stoppered her words with embarrassment in any other situation. "Kiss me while I ride you."

"You have no idea how fucking sexy it is that you know exactly what you want." He scooted back enough that she could brace her knees on the mattress. Then he hooked one arm around her waist while he dug his other hand into her hair. He tugged a little. "Yes?"

She moaned. "Yes." She loved when Gideon didn't treat her like she was breakable. He didn't so much as hesitate when she urged him to bite her harder, to grab her tighter. Things she hadn't even known she craved until he gave them to her.

Lucy slid down until he was completely sheathed inside her. She had to pause to adjust to the almost uncomfortable fullness. The sensation passed quickly, dissipating to sheer pleasure as her body accommodated his size. She wrapped her arms around his shoulders and kissed him as she started to move. Their position had him rubbing against her clit with every stroke and, despite trying to hold out, her orgasm loomed all too soon.

Her strokes went choppy. *"Gideon."*

He shifted his hands to her hips, helping her maintain the rhythm that would get her where she needed to go. "You feel so fucking good."

"You…too." She opened her eyes, not sure when she'd closed them, and the expression on his face stilled her breath in her lungs. *Possession. Desire. Need.* It was too much.

Lucy cried out his name as she came. He kept her moving, kept the orgasm going, until her muscles gave out and she slumped against him.

He carefully pulled out of her and shifted them back onto the bed. Gideon spooned her, lightly stroking her arm, her hip, her stomach. She stared at the art print on the wall next to her bed for several long moments while she relearned how to breathe. Gradually she became aware of a very specific part of him pressed against her ass. "You didn't come."

"Not yet."

Not yet.

Who knew those two little words would be the sexiest thing she'd ever heard?

Gideon kept up his light touching until Lucy arched back against him. Judging her to be recovered enough, he hooked one knee and lifted her leg up and over his legs, leaving her open to him. He slid a hand carefully between her thighs, testing her tenderness. "Tell me what you want."

"You."

He kissed the back of her neck. "You have me." *For now.* "Tell me what other fantasies you've been harboring." The image of her using that toy on herself would be enough to keep him up at night for the foreseeable future. He was a goddamn idiot for feeding his imagination more images, but he craved them the same way he craved her.

"You want my sexual bucket list?" Her amused tone turned into a gasp as he idly stroked her clit. "You can't expect me to think when you're doing *that.*"

"Consider it inspiration." He liked the idea of being the one who helped her cross items off that type of list. Fuck, he liked the thought that he was in her bed right now and would be for as long as she felt he had something to teach her.

Lucy reached back to sift her fingers through his hair. "I haven't really thought about it."

"Liar." He took the move for an invitation and slid his other arm beneath her so he could palm her breasts. "There's at least a few things you have lurking in the back of your mind about this—something you've always wanted to try." Something he could be the only one to ever give to her.

At least for now.

She hesitated and he could practically hear her thinking it over and considering laying herself bare in this way. Gideon could have pointed out that they were already bared to each other, but this was different.

He stilled his hands, waiting for her answer.

"Don't stop." She covered the hand between her legs with one of her own, guiding him back to her clit and then lower, to push a finger inside her. Lucy moaned. "High-end dressing room. I've always wanted to have sex in a high-end dressing room—lingerie, maybe, if that's not super cliché." She tensed. "Crap. I'm doing it again. God, it's so hard to turn *off*."

"I think we could make that happen." He kissed along her neck to growl in her ear. "I want to see you in green—that bright jewel tone."

She tilted her head forward, giving him better access. "I think we could make that happen." She echoed his words back to him.

"Charitable of you." He paused his stroking long enough to guide his cock into her. She clamped tight around him and he barely bit back a curse.

As many times as he'd slipped and imagined what it would be like to have Lucy in his bed, his fantasies hadn't come close to the bliss of reality. She was fucking perfection. Every move, every word, every gasp—Gideon stored them all away in his memory. He only had a limited time to accumulate enough to last him a lifetime.

A worry for another day.

Tonight he was inside Lucy.

Tomorrow could wait until tomorrow.

Gideon sat in Lucy's living room and ate reheated leftovers. She had a bright throw wrapped around her shoulders and her cat in her lap as she tried to arrange her food in an order that she could actually eat. He reached over and plucked the cat out of her lap.

Or he tried.

In reality, Garfunkel had no intention of going anywhere against his will. He let loose a yowl that raised the small hairs on the back of Gideon's neck. Before he could react, the cat hissed and swiped claws across his forearm. He cursed but managed not to chuck the horrid little beast. Instead he dropped the animal the short distance to the floor.

"Oh, my God!" Lucy shoved her food containers to the side and grabbed his wrist. "What were you thinking?"

He gritted his teeth as she dabbed at the blood welling in the scratches with a napkin. "I was thinking you'd have an easier time eating if he wasn't taking up so much space on your lap."

"You weren't wrong." She dabbed a little harder. "But if you haven't noticed, Garfunkel is territorial. And he doesn't like men much."

"You think?" He took the napkin from her and pressed it hard against his arm. "It's fine. I should have known better." His lifestyle wasn't one that allowed for a pet, but if it had, Gideon would definitely be a dog person. Cats seemed to be little assholes as a general rule, and he had a feeling if he tried to adopt one, he'd pick the biggest asshole of them all through sheer karma.

Though Garfunkel has a solid running for that title.

"I'm really sorry."

"Lucy, it's fine." He grabbed his food and joined her on the couch. "How are you feeling?"

"Unwound." She leaned her head against the back of the couch and gave him a sleepy smile. "I'd forgotten how relaxing good sex could be."

Good doesn't begin to cover it.

He bit the comment back. It was sheer pride that made him want to say it and he didn't have a right. Not in the current situation. He was here for a specific purpose and he couldn't afford to forget that even for a moment. Lucy wasn't for him in any permanent way. This was a window into the world of what could have been in another life, if things had fallen out in a different sequence of events.

But they hadn't. So here he and Lucy were.

"What made you pick those particular men?"

It took him a few seconds too long to make the subject change with her. He didn't want to talk about other men while he still had the memory of her body against his and the smell of her on his skin. It felt wrong on a whole hell of a lot of different levels. An intrusion.

Except it wasn't.

Lucy had asked him for a specific set of things, and sex had been an afterthought. Just because it wasn't an afterthought for Gideon didn't mean he could snap at her for keeping her head in the game. So he did his best to do the same.

"They're all ambitious men who have reputations for being honest and are old enough that they're likely thinking about settling down with one person. I've personally placed both Mark and Liam in jobs, so I did all the research and then some. They have solid histories. Neither has any record of being a cheater or abusive in any way. They're good guys—as good as anyone is." And he'd checked. Even with only twenty-four hours at his disposal, he'd done extensive research and even gone so far as to call a few of their exes, though Gideon wasn't about to admit that to Lucy. None of the women had said anything to raise red flags.

She speared a green bean with her fork. "And Aaron?"

"He's the best of the best. I actually tried to poach him for a client last year and he wouldn't give me the time of day." When she raised her eyebrows, he shifted, something like embarrassment sifting through him. "There's more to it than that, of course. He's got an excellent reputation, and Roman is actually friends with him."

"Your pitch is overwhelming." She laughed softly. "But then, this is what I asked for, isn't it?"

He didn't like seeing that look on her face, as if she was resigning herself to a life half lived. "Lucy, if you want to change directions on this thing, we can do that. Even if you go on dates with these guys, nothing is set in stone."

"I know you mean well, but I would very much appreciate it if you'd stop trying to talk me out of this."

He tried to rein in his temper, but he'd held himself too tightly under control the last two days. Too careful. It wasn't Gideon's natural default, and it had started to wear on him. He glared. "I'm not trying to talk you out of shit. I'm giving you options. You want this to have a chance in hell of working, you need to stop being so goddamn defensive. I'm helping you with this bat-shit-crazy plan, so I need you to throw me a bone once in a while."

She set down her fork. "I think you should leave."

Fuck. He started to apologize but stopped. Lucy might be fragile in some ways, but she wasn't broken. He had to remember that and stop treating her with kid gloves. And yet letting her make what might be the biggest mistake of her life because he felt guilty over her last relationship was a shitty thing to do.

He wasn't sure what his other options were, but he'd have to figure it out. Fast.

In the meantime he needed to get the hell out of there before he said something they'd both regret. Gideon stood and buttoned the last few buttons on his shirt. "I'll email you the details tomorrow."

"Okay." She still wouldn't look at him.

He hesitated, but there was nothing left to say. Sex had changed things. Having concrete proof of how deep the connection ran between them was enough to set him back on his heels. She felt it, too. There was no way she didn't.

Now he just needed her to actually admit it.

CHAPTER SEVEN

"I'M SORRY—did you just say that you have a *date*?"

Lucy swirled her white wine, not looking at her little sister. "You don't have to sound so shocked by it." She hadn't wanted to confess her plan, but it twisted her up inside not to be able to talk about it with at least one person. Gideon hardly counted, especially since his reactions were hardly consistent with what she'd expected—and *her* reactions weren't cooperating, either.

"I *am* shocked. You've been all work, work, work. When did you have time to set up a date?" Becka leaned over and snagged a chip from the plate in the middle of the table. "That's not a dig, by the way. That's just facts. I'm on three freaking dating websites and *I* have trouble finding dates who aren't candidates for 'but he seemed so nice.'"

Lucy sighed. "They can't all be serial killers, Becka."

"It only takes one." Becka frowned. "Besides, we aren't talking about me. We're talking about you."

Now that push came to shove, she didn't know where to start. Or if she even should confess any of it. In truth, if she hadn't had these drinks set up with Becka already, she'd be at home, moping. It had been two days since she'd seen Gideon and, aside from a few emails confirming her first date, they hadn't talked, either. She knew she'd been an ass, but it wasn't like Gideon to avoid a conflict.

Not that there had to be a conflict. There didn't. She just didn't want him to think that their having sex meant he could push her into not going through with her plan. She'd made the decision. He had to respect that. If that meant he didn't want to continue with their lessons… Well, that was something she'd just have to deal with.

Unless he doesn't want to continue for a different reason...

"You okay?"

She blinked and tried to focus on her sister's face. Becka changed her hair color with the seasons and today it was a bright blue that was the exact shade of her eyes. Her lip piercing glinted in the light of the little hipster bar where they always met up. She had the cute-alternative look down to a science. *She* never had problems with men, despite her lamenting about dating.

Lucy tried to smile. "Just a crisis of faith. You know, the usual."

"Don't do that. If you don't want to tell me, that's cool, but don't pat me on the head. You don't have to protect me anymore, Lucy. You know that, right?"

"It's not about protecting you." And it wasn't. They'd had a fine upbringing. Decent—if distant—

parents. A solid middle-class lifestyle. Nothing traumatic happening to make waves in their lives.

But Becka was still her little sister. When they were growing up, Becka had been the shy one, the bookworm who was a little too odd to fit in with the rest of the kids in her grade. It led to bullying and, when their parents had failed to notice, Lucy had taken care of it.

She'd been taking care of her little sister ever since.

Though these days, Becka fought her own battles.

But her sister had a point. Holding on to the turmoil inside her wasn't doing Lucy any favors. She'd talked about it to Gideon, but he wasn't exactly a neutral party. Neither was Becka, for that matter. "I just… I know it's been two years, but I still have Jeff's comments rattling around in my brain. It's pathetic and I should be over it by now, and I *am* over *him*. I don't know what's wrong with me."

"Nothing's wrong with you." Becka grabbed the wine bottle on the table and refilled her glass. "It's not like you had a monthlong relationship and turned around and let it mess you up for the rest of your life. You and Jeff were together for…what, like four years? You were going to marry him." She narrowed her blue eyes. "Though he better hope we never cross paths, because I'm going to kick his ass one of these days."

"Becka."

"Lucy." She mimicked her voice perfectly. "But that day is not today. Either way, I'd say you were having a normal reaction and that's that. Why's this coming up now? The whole matchmaking thing is kind of out there, but it's not like you're jumping into bed with these guys to give them a trial run." Becka grinned. "Though *there's* an idea."

She tried to imagine it—taking a single night with each of the guys on Gideon's list—and instantly rejected the idea. "No way." It felt wrong and she didn't want to spend too much time thinking about why. *I promised Gideon to be exclusive.* Sure, that was it. Definitely.

"Worth a shot." Becka ate a few more chips. "You'll be fine, Lucy. I promise. Dating is weird and it's hard to get to know people, but you have a matchmaker in your corner. It'll all work out."

She couldn't tell her sister that Gideon Novak was the so-called matchmaker in question. Becka had met him on several occasions and she'd lose her shit if she knew. Since they'd managed to get through this conversation without her thinking Lucy was out of her mind, she'd like to keep it that way. "I'm sure you're right."

"I am."

Lucy's phone rang and her heart leaped in her throat at the sight of Gideon's name on the screen. "Hello?"

"I'll meet you there ten minutes early, so be ready."

She blinked. "I'm sorry—what?"

"The date, Lucy. Please tell me you haven't forgotten about it."

She bristled at the irritation in his voice. "Of course I haven't forgotten. But I was not expecting you to be attending." She was nervous enough about going out with Mark Williams without having to do it under the watchful eye of Gideon. "That's unacceptable."

"My rules. Be there ten minutes early." He hung up.

Lucy set her phone carefully on the table and looked up to find her sister watching her. "What?"

"I know that move. The 'gently set your phone down so you don't chuck it across the room' one. Who pissed you off?"

"It's a long story and, unfortunately, I have to leave in order not to be late." *Not to be late to being early. I'm going to kill him.* She dug out her wallet and flagged down the waitress. "Same time next week?"

"Sure. You're the one with the crazy schedule." Becka finished her drink and set it on the table. She grinned. "And whoever that was that just called you, give 'em hell, sis."

"I plan on it." She set the appropriate amount of cash on the table under the ticket and rose. She accepted Gideon's direction in the bedroom because that was exactly what she'd asked for. She accepted his list of men for the same reason.

She refused to accept him taking control of every aspect of this matchmaking situation.

He vetted and picked the candidates, yes, but ultimately it was up to her and the individual men to see if it was something that could actually work. Gideon's role in this ended the second she and one of the men came to an agreement. She tried very hard not to focus on the way her stomach dropped at that thought.

It didn't matter.

What mattered was his trying to steamroll her on

this. She had to have some freedom to figure out if she could stomach the thought of spending her life with the man across the table from her, and she couldn't do that with Gideon standing at her shoulder.

If he did, she couldn't shake the feeling that she'd compare every man to him and it would skew her perception.

Against Gideon Novak, who could compare?

Gideon checked his watch for the third time in as many minutes. Where the hell was she? He turned to look down the street again just as Lucy walked around the corner. She didn't seem particularly concerned to be running late—or happy to see him. He motioned to his watch. "We had an understanding."

"Wrong. You told me something. I disagreed." She crossed her arms over her chest, which drew his attention to her dress.

"What are you wearing?" It was a pale blue lacy thing that gave the illusion of showing more than it actually did. It clung to her body, the gaps in the lace showing a nude lining the exact same shade as her skin. At a glance, she might as well have been naked beneath it.

He loved it.

He fucking hated it.

"A dress." She touched it, a frown drawing a line between her brows. "Don't take that overprotective tone with me, Gideon. It's a good dress."

"It's inappropriate for a first date. He's going to sit

across that table and spend the whole time thinking about fucking you."

Lucy gave him a brilliant grin, her plum-colored lips mirroring the darkness of her hair, which she'd left in waves down around her shoulders. "Then it's doing its job. Now, if you'd please get out of my way, I can take it from here." She strode past him and through the door to the restaurant.

Jealousy flared, hot and poisonous, down the back of his throat. He didn't have a right to it any more now than he had before, but it was a thousand times more powerful now that they'd put sex on the table. Gideon followed her inside and hooked a hand around her elbow, towing her sideways into a small hallway that led to the coat check.

It was dimmer there than in the main entrance—more intimate. He pressed his hands to the wall on either side of her shoulders. "You make me fucking crazy."

"That makes two of us." She poked him in the chest. "You might be calling the shots in some things, but you have to give me enough space to breathe. The compressed timeline is already going to play havoc on my instincts—I don't need your constant presence doing the same."

He'd think about how his presence affected her later. Right now all he could focus on was the first part of the sentence. "If the timeline is too tight, then extend it. The only person who put this deadline in place was *you*."

"And it stands." She lifted her chin. "I'm already

late for this date. I don't want to have this conversation for the seventh time. Just give me some space to breathe."

He pushed off the wall even though it was the last thing he wanted to do. The truth was that he wanted Lucy, and it was fucking up his head space and messing with *his* instincts. He knew better than to push her, but he couldn't help doing it all the same. He wanted her and she wanted him—at least physically.

What if it could be more than just physical?

What if I actually played for keeps?

The thought stopped him in his tracks.

He watched Lucy greet the hostess and follow her deeper into the restaurant, but he couldn't move. This whole time, he had been letting Lucy take the wheel and guide things—at least to some extent. Gideon had handled her so goddamn carefully because he was well aware of the damage Jeff had caused her and he blamed himself, at least a little, because of it. That guilt was the same reason he hadn't pushed her to face the fact that there was more than just friendship between them.

But what if he did?

He couldn't hit this head-on—Lucy would tell him to get lost, and with good reason. She had her eye on the prize and she wouldn't be deterred by an outside force, even if it was Gideon.

If he could get her to change her mind, that would be a different story.

Gideon smiled.

Let her have her date with Mark. The guy was nice

enough, but Gideon fully intended to take her to bed until she was so wrapped up in him that she forgot Mark's fucking name.

A man looked up as Lucy approached the table the hostess had indicated. He was cute in a hipster sort of way, his close-cropped beard and glasses a combination that would have been strange five years before. Now it seemed like everyone had them. The only thing missing was suspenders or a bow tie. Instead, he wore a nice button-up shirt and a pair of slacks. When he rose to pull her chair out for her, she got an eyeful of his broad shoulders and clearly outlined muscles.

Too many muscles. Too much facial hair.

Oh, my God, stop. *What is wrong with me?*

He resumed his place and grinned at her, his teeth white and straight. "Lucy, I presume. Otherwise, this is about to get incredibly awkward."

That startled a laugh out of her. "Yes, I'm Lucy." She extended her hand. "That would make you Mark."

"The very one." He gave her a firm handshake, which she appreciated. Too many men—especially men who worked in corporate jobs—tended to give handshakes like they thought they'd break her. It drove her crazy.

Mark leaned back, his gaze roaming over her face. *Another mark in his favor—not ogling my chest.* Lucy gave herself a shake. She had to stop overanalyzing every second of this date. Mark was most definitely not Gideon, and that didn't have to be a tally in the negative column.

It was just hard to focus when she could still smell Gideon's cologne from where he'd pressed her against the wall a few short minutes ago. It wasn't musky and strong like so many men she knew—it was light and clean and reminded her of… She couldn't place it.

Focus.

She gave a polite smile. "Thank you for agreeing to the date."

"When Gideon called me and explained the situation, I'll admit I didn't believe him." The corner of his mouth hitched up. "And then I asked him what was wrong with you."

She tensed and then admonished herself for doing so. He was joking. He didn't really think there was something wrong with her. "As you can see, I'm in possession of all my teeth."

"Not to mention beautiful and successful." Mark's easy smile made the words fact rather than a throw-away compliment. "I've heard of marriages of convenience, but I assumed they were the stuff of fiction. This whole situation is kind of strange."

"I can't argue that." She'd known it was a reach the second she'd called Gideon to put the plan into action. That didn't change the fact that she had no other option. "But I have to ask. If you think it's so strange, why are you here?"

He sighed. "I'm fucking up this small talk, aren't I? That was way too heavy to start in on."

"I don't mind. This isn't exactly the most conventional situation." She appreciated the frankness, even if there was something missing from this interaction that she couldn't quite put her finger on. Mark was attractive—there was no denying that—but… Lucy didn't know. It was off.

"In that case, I agreed to this because I've worked eighty-hour weeks for several years and that won't be stopping anytime soon. I don't know if you've been to a bar lately, but meeting people there is a joke. Everyone is on their phones or with their friends or not interested. Dating apps are even worse, in large part because women have so many nightmare encounters that they're edgy and distant. It makes it hard to really get to know a person when they're sure that you're going to turn on a dime and send a dick pic or freak out because they cancel the date." He shrugged. "It comes down to time. I don't have much of it to meet new people and jump through the hoops of first dates and second dates—and balancing the knife edge of showing that I'm interested without being too goddamn pushy." Mark sighed. "Sorry. It's a sore spot for me."

There was a story there—perhaps several.

The waitress appeared to take their order and then disappeared as quickly. Lucy leaned forward. "Tell me some of your dating stories."

He raised his eyebrows. "If there was a playbook for first dates, I'm one hundred percent sure it wouldn't include recalling dates with other women."

"This is hardly your textbook first date." She smiled. "My little sister runs the gauntlet of online dating, and some of her stories defy belief."

"I wish I could say she was making it all up." Mark relaxed a little, just the slight loosening in his shoulders. She hadn't realized he was tense until it disappeared. He grinned. "If she's half as beautiful as you, she's seen more than her fair share of crazy on those sites."

"I'm sure she has." Lucy knew all too well that Becka had kept plenty of it back, sharing only the funny stories. That was what gave her away—there only seemed to be funny stories. Nothing dark, nothing worrisome. Nothing indicating she'd met anyone she had more than a passing interest for. "Tell me about them."

He hesitated, surveying her expression, but he must have seen only the interest she felt there because he chuckled. "I'd rather know more about you. Gideon said you're a lawyer."

"I'm a defense attorney." She had to wonder what else Gideon had told Mark and the other men he'd managed to get to agree to meet her. Lucy looked good on paper. She was confident in that, even if she wasn't in any other romantic aspect of her life.

But a lot of women looked good on paper and weren't going about marriage in such an odd way.

Mark leaned forward, expression attentive. "Do you like it? I've been fascinated with the court system since I was a kid. Too many *Law & Order* marathons, you know."

"It's not much like that in real life. There's a truly unglamorous amount of paperwork, and research can be tedious to the point where I've believed more than once that it might kill me." She forced herself to relax a little. "But actually being in court is exhilarating. It's like a game of chess but with higher stakes. I wouldn't trade it for the world."

Their food arrived and the conversation proceeded easily, her work moving into his work as cybersecurity expert, and then sharing a bit about their childhoods. Mark was as nice as he was handsome and Lucy waited through the entire meal for her heartbeat to pick up at the sight of his smile, or for her mind to leapfrog into what it would be like to get naked with him.

There was nothing but a vague pleasant feeling of spending her time in friendly conversation.

No sizzle whatsoever.

She'd asked for that, but she couldn't help comparing him to Gideon. They were different in so many ways. Mark was built lean like a blade—a very well-muscled blade—whereas Gideon looked like a Viking who had decided he'd bring his pillaging to the corporate world. His broad shoulders created a V that tapered down to a narrow waist and there was no way he'd be able to buy a suit off the rack with those powerful thighs.

Mark was attractive but missing a vital component she couldn't put her finger on. A sizzle. A flair. Something that screamed *life*.

I've been reading too many romance novels.

Or maybe she was trying to rationalize something that couldn't be rationalized. She didn't have a connection with Mark. That didn't mean there was something wrong with her—or with him. It just wasn't there.

Mark seemed to notice it, as well. He paid for their meal and sat back with a rueful smile. "This has been fun, but I won't be hearing from you for a second date, will I?"

She liked his frankness. She just wished she felt some kind of pull to the match.

Lucy pressed her lips together. "I can't say for certain."

"I get it." He stood and moved around the table to pull out her chair. "I'd love to get to know you better—as friends."

That was exactly it. She'd enjoyed the dinner. She wouldn't mind spending more time with him. She just couldn't imagine walking down the aisle to him, even in an arranged setting. "Thank you for a wonderful evening."

Mark pressed a quick kiss to her cheek. "You're something special, Lucy Baudin. I hope you get what you're looking for."

"You, too. She's out there. Don't give up yet."

He squeezed her hand. "Good night, Lucy."

She followed him to the door and allowed him to hail her a cab. It was only when she was on her way back to her apartment that she took out her phone and texted Gideon.

Heading home.

I'll be there in thirty.

Her stomach dipped pleasantly and she clenched her thighs together. There was no mistaking what would happen the second he walked through her door, and her skin heated just thinking about it.

She couldn't wait.

CHAPTER EIGHT

GIDEON STORMED THROUGH Lucy's door without knocking. He found her pacing nervously around her living room, practically wringing her hands, and stopped short. "What did he do?"

Her blue eyes went wide. "Excuse me?"

"Mark. Obviously he did something." He sliced his hand through the air to indicate her current state. "Tell me what it was and I'll take care of it." He'd thought Mark was a safe enough bet for the first date, but Gideon shouldn't have taken it for granted. If he'd stayed, he could've stepped in.

Lucy was still blinking at him. She burst out laughing. "Mark was a perfect gentleman."

"You don't have to smooth it over. It's my job to ensure you have solid dates, and if something went wrong, I need to know." He very pointedly ignored the fact that he almost hoped something had ruined the night. Mark was fucking perfect. If he wasn't essentially married to his job, he would have found a girl, gotten married and had a couple of kids by now.

She crossed to him and put a hand on his chest.

"Gideon, stop. Nothing happened. We had a nice conversation and decided to leave things at that."

Leave things at that.

Call him crazy, but he hadn't spent much time dwelling on what would transpire during—and after—the dates. Jealousy reared its ugly head and, even as he fought for control, his words got away from him. "Did he hold your hand?"

She blinked. "I don't know if I'd call it hand-holding—"

"Help you into your coat?" He took a step closer to her, crowding her and unable to stop. "Kiss you?" The thought of Mark in Gideon's current position, leaning down to take Lucy's mouth, made him crazy.

And, damn it, she saw it.

Lucy frowned. "What's wrong?"

"Nothing." *Fucking everything.* He kissed her to keep from saying anything else. Lucy responded instantly, her hands sliding up his chest to loop her arms around his neck, her body melting into his. Her instant yielding should have soothed him.

There were far too many "shoulds" when it came to Lucy Baudin.

He grabbed the hem of her dress and yanked it up as he tumbled her back onto the couch. Gideon had the presence of mind to catch himself so she didn't bear the full brunt of his weight. The break in their kiss gave him the chance to say, "You want this."

"That wasn't a question. But yes." She jerked his shirt out of his pants and went to work on the buttons. "I want to feel you."

He palmed her pussy. "Then feel me." He spread her and pushed a single finger into her. Lucy made one of those sexy fucking whimpers that he couldn't get enough of and yanked his shirt apart, sending the last few buttons flying.

She shoved the shirt down his shoulders. "I need you, Gideon."

He'd give every single dollar he owned to hear her say those words every single day of his life. It wasn't his destiny, but he sure as hell planned to coax her to say it as often as he could during their time together. "Tell me. Guide me."

"I, uh..." Her eyes shut for a split second as he circled her clit with his thumb. When she opened them again, there was new purpose there. "I want you in my mouth."

He froze. "Lucy—" *Fuck me, it's like she pulled a fantasy right out of my goddamn head.* He saw the exact moment her confidence wavered and bit back a curse. He was so determined to give her everything, he was missing signs.

Gideon shifted to sit next to her on the couch. He stopped her from going to the floor with a hand on her shoulder. "Open my pants."

She didn't hesitate. Lucy undid the front of his slacks and withdrew his cock. She stroked him once and then sucked him into her mouth. Gideon had expected some sort of cautious exploration, but she went after it like she was desperate for him.

As desperate for him as he was for her. He pulled her hair back so he could see his cock disappear between her deep purple lips. A sight he never thought he'd stand witness to. She opened her eyes and pinned him with a pleased look, and he couldn't stand it a second longer. Keeping one hand holding her hair back, Gideon pulled her dress higher, baring her ass completely. He squeezed her ass and then ran his hand down until he could push two fingers into her.

Her eyes went wide then slid shut and she sucked him harder, faster.

"You like that? You like me playing with your pretty pussy while you have my cock in your mouth." It wasn't enough. He was so goddamn desperate for her that feeling her come on his fingers wouldn't do a thing to take the edge off. He kept thinking about her wearing that peekaboo dress across the table from Mark and laughing at that fucker's jokes, and inspiring a lifetime of filthy fantasies. "Give me a taste."

He grabbed her around the hips and lifted her until her knees rested on the back of the couch on either side of his head. Gideon waited for her to start sucking his cock again before he ran his cheek up her thigh to her pussy. "So beautiful." He licked her, teasing.

Or at least that was the plan.

She was so fucking drenched and tasted so fucking sweet, he lost his precarious hold on his control and gripped her thighs where they met her hips, raising her to his mouth and spreading her wider in the same move. She moaned around his cock and the sound drove him wilder. He licked and sucked her folds, growling against her hot skin. *I've got my face bur-*

ied in her pussy. Me. *Not that asshole she went to dinner with.*

Lucy reached between his thighs and cupped his balls, slamming him back into the present. She twisted up off his cock enough to say, "You like this?"

"Hell, yes, I do. I like every single thing you do to me." His world narrowed down to the taste of her on his tongue and the feel of her mouth wrapped around him. Her whimpers and moans drove him on, leaching every bit of rational thought from Gideon's head. He needed her to orgasm.

Needed to claim her.

Lucy couldn't tell which way was up—and not just because Gideon had her in the most impossible and erotic position. She'd barely made it home before him and now he had her upside down on the couch with his face buried between her legs as she sucked his cock. She took him deeper. He made her so damn crazy.

For once, she wanted to return the favor.

She shifted her hold of his balls, squeezing lightly. He made a sound she felt all the way to the back of her throat. Nothing mattered but the next slide of his tongue over her clit and the way his fingers dug into her hips, effortlessly holding her in place.

Her orgasm rolled over her from one breath to the next, and she sucked him with unmatched desperation, needing Gideon with her every step of the way. She could *feel* him holding back, trying to outlast her just like he had every other time since they'd started.

If she didn't do something drastic right this second, he'd move them somewhere else and she wouldn't get a chance to finish him like this.

So she played dirty.

Lucy pressed two fingers to his perineum. She'd read in so many books that it was a hot spot for men as well as women, but she'd never had the courage to try.

Gideon's response made the risk worth it many times over.

His back arched and his balls drew up. He hissed out a breath that made her clit tingle. "Fuck. I can't hold out."

She sucked harder, not willing to lift her head to tell him to go for it. She wanted this. She *needed* this.

He hesitated but she circled her middle finger against him and that was all it took. Gideon cursed long and hard against her skin, his grip spasming as his hips bucked up to meet her mouth. She took him as deep as was comfortable and then took him deeper yet. He growled her name as he came. Lucy drank him down, sucking him until he shuddered and gently lowered her to the couch.

Only then did she raise her head.

The look on Gideon's face could only be described as shell-shocked. He opened his mouth, closed it and shook his head. "Come here." Without waiting for a response, he pulled her onto his lap and tucked her against him.

She settled her head onto his shoulder. "That was..."

"Yeah."

How to put it into words? She might not be the more experienced of the two of them, but she wasn't stupid. That hadn't been like the other times. There was no lesson here that Gideon wanted to teach her. He'd come through her door like a jealous boyfriend and then delivered one of the most devastating orgasms of her life and now he was holding her like he…cared.

Of course he cares. He wouldn't have agreed to this if he didn't.

Just because he considered her a friend didn't mean the lines had blurred for him.

She clung to the thought with a stubbornness born of desperation. Lucy had a plan and she knew better by now than to deviate from it. The last time she'd done that, she'd ended up with Jeff, and that entire experience had screwed her up, at least emotionally.

It would have screwed her up professionally, too, if she processed pain in any other way than powering through it out of spite.

Gideon stroked a hand down her back. "Did I hurt you?"

"What? No." She leaned back to look at him. Not as shell-shocked now and the thread of guilt in his dark eyes made her heart hurt.

That was the other reason she couldn't allow the lines between them to blur. Gideon might be someone she cared about, and he might make her body sing, but he would never forgive himself for his role in Jeff's shitty choices.

He'd never be able to look at her without seeing his

friend's ex-fiancée. The one *he'd* had to take aside to let know she was being cheated on—and everyone knew.

Gideon frowned. "Tell me what put that look on your face."

"It's nothing." The very *last* thing she wanted to do was to bring Jeff into the room with them. It was hard enough to banish the memory of him without inviting him in. She almost settled back against Gideon, but the moment had passed. Cuddling and soft words wasn't what this was.

Lucy climbed to her feet on shaking legs. "Give me a few minutes to change."

"Sure."

She retreated to her bedroom and threw on a pair of leggings and one of her knitted sweaters. It felt too comfortable, but as he'd been quick to point out before, this wasn't about seduction. If he wanted her to dress the part, he would request it so he could help her strike the right note. She closed her bedroom door behind her and made her way back into the main room. "I need to go shopping."

"This instant?"

"Don't be silly. Of course not." Her laugh felt forced, mostly because it was. Lucy pulled a newly purchased bottle of wine out of her cabinet and took out two glasses. "Wine?"

"Yeah."

She poured them, still not looking at him. "The date with Mark was nice enough, but I think it's best I meet the rest of your list. That said, I'd like to be as prepared as possible, and I think I mentioned before that I have nothing in the way of seduction clothing."

Gideon snorted. "*You* are seduction enough, Lucy."

He didn't get it. But then, she didn't expect him to. She turned and offered his glass then took a sip of her own. "This may sound strange, but I dress well."

"I noticed."

She ignored that. "Walking out to face a judge or jury—or both—is terrifying. It's exhilarating, too, but taking that first step is like jumping out of a plane and hoping you remembered your parachute. Or, more accurately maybe, it's like stepping onto the dueling grounds and hoping like hell you prepared your weapons and they won't malfunction. I know that sounds dramatic, but it's what it feels like for me. My clothing is both armor and weapons combined. It allows me to take that first step without fear crippling me. I'm going to need that in the bedroom, as well."

There. He might laugh in her face, but at least she was being honest.

Gideon didn't laugh. He studied her with those dark eyes, mulling over what she said and the implications behind it, no doubt. She'd revealed far more of herself in that little tidbit than she had in a long while. Becka knew, of course—she was the one Lucy always dragged along on her shopping trips—but everyone at the office assumed that Lucy was just extremely into fashion and expensive clothing.

Finally he took a drink of his wine. "Do you have free time next weekend?"

Next weekend? It was Thursday. "That's eight days from now."

"I'm more than capable of counting, Lucy." He set the glass down. "Tomorrow, you'll meet Aaron Livingston at the weekly event Roman puts together. I'll be out of town most of next week meeting with several potential fits for a client."

Disappointment soured her stomach but she did her best not to show it. Of course Gideon wasn't exclusively focused on her predicament. From what she remembered, he usually had multiple clients at any given time and there was no reason to expect to be the exception to the rule.

It also meant almost a full week that she wouldn't see him.

No lessons for seven days.

Stop it.

She managed a smile. "I'm free next weekend, aside from a lunch date with Becka."

"We'll go shopping afterward."

Which would give her a chance to imbibe enough alcohol to feel a little fearless at the thought of picking lingerie with Gideon. Lucy wasn't feeling anything resembling fearless at the moment. She swallowed hard. "Okay."

His gaze sharpened on her face. "Tomorrow, wear something appropriate."

Just like that, her nerves disappeared. She drew herself up straight. "Excuse me?"

"You know damn well that you were playing with fire with that dress tonight. I don't know how the fuck

Mark kept his hands to himself, but it's a small miracle. No other man would."

Meaning *he* wouldn't, which he'd more than proved by walking through the door and ravishing her right there in her living room. *I did a bit of ravishing myself.*

That wasn't what they were discussing, though, and she didn't appreciate his attitude. The whole point of this was to market her—for lack of a better word—to these men, and he was acting like she'd been out of line. It wasn't a dress she would have worn for work, but it was a far cry from indecent. He was acting like she'd shown up in a minidress with all her goods on display. Lucy glared. "I'll wear whatever I please."

"Wrong. You'll wear something that doesn't project sex."

"You can't be serious." She threw up a hand. "I am more than capable of dressing myself. The lingerie excepting, I don't need or want your opinion."

Gideon set the wineglass down and advanced on her, a forbidding expression on his handsome face. A muscle in his jaw jumped and her stomach leaped in response. He stopped mere inches away. "You wear some shit like you wore tonight and you won't like the results."

She could barely catch her breath with him so close. "What are you going to do, Gideon? Put me over your knee? I don't think so."

"Put you over my knee." His hands came down on either side of her, bracketing her in. Still, he didn't touch her. "Yes, Lucy, that's exactly what I'll do. And after I've spanked your pert little ass red, I'll bend you over the nearest surface and fuck you, date with another man or no."

CHAPTER NINE

"YOU KEEP STARING at the door like that, you're going to start scaring guests away."

Gideon didn't look away from the door. He couldn't relax. Truth be told, he hadn't managed to relax since he'd walked out of Lucy's apartment last night, his words ringing in his ears. They hadn't talked today, other than his text with the address and time to be here and her reply that she would show up.

The question of *how* she would show up was driving him crazy.

He didn't know which outcome he wanted. It would be best if Lucy listened to him and dressed in something that was less of a goddamn tease.

But a part of him wanted her to challenge him—to push him to follow through on his threat. It crossed the line and he knew it, but he was past caring. If Lucy's date with Mark had made anything clear, it was that Gideon couldn't stand the thought of her with another man.

He'd stepped aside for Jeff.

He wasn't about to step aside now. Not again.

None of those other fuckers would care about her the way he would. Their chemistry about set the apartment on fire, and they had a history of genuine caring between them—all of which Lucy said she wanted with whatever husband she picked.

He was the right choice.

He just had to find a way to make Lucy see that.

"Shit," Roman muttered. He stepped to the side, blocking Gideon's view of the door. "Don't make a scene. I invited Aaron here in good faith and you look like you're about to rip someone's head off if they glance at you wrong."

"I'm not going to make a scene." As long as Lucy didn't test him.

He hoped like hell she *did* test him.

"The expression on your face is about to make a liar out of you." Roman slid his hands into his pockets, still looking on edge. "You've already crossed the line with Lucy, haven't you?"

He'd crossed so many lines, he'd lost count. But Roman wasn't bringing this up now just for shits and giggles. Gideon jerked his chin to the side. "Get out of the way."

"No. Scene."

Roman stepped out of the way and Gideon went still. Lucy made her way through the tables toward the VIP section, drawing stares in her wake. She had on a little black dress, but to call it that didn't do it justice. It was so short, it made her already long legs look even longer. It was also strapless, the heart-shaped bodice adding extra curves to her body. Her hair was down in a carefully messy wave that made him think of fucking, and her bloodred mouth only drove the image of hot sex home. She nodded at the guy manning the entrance to the VIP section and then strode straight to Gideon. Closer, he realized there were little beads sewn into the skirt of the dress, giving an extra shift of movement with each step.

Without looking away from Lucy, he handed Roman his beer. "We'll be right back."

Roman cursed. "Whatever you're going to say to her, make it quick. Aaron will be here in thirty."

Thirty minutes was more than enough time to thoroughly make his point. He stood and prowled the last few steps to her. "Follow me. Now."

She wet her lips, her eyes already a little hazy. "And if I don't want to?"

"You do." He turned and stalked back through the VIP section to the hallway that led to bathrooms and two rooms for meetings or private parties. One held a table and chairs and Gideon had used it on more than one occasion. The other had several couches for a more informal touch.

He chose the boardroom.

He opened the door and walked in, Lucy on his heels. She shut the door behind her and glared. "This is ridiculous."

"If you really thought that, you wouldn't be here right now." He grabbed her hips and pulled her against him. She instantly went soft, even as her blue eyes sparked. Gideon dipped his hands beneath her dress and froze. "What the fuck, Lucy?"

"Hmm?"

"You know exactly what I'm talking about." He pulled her dress up, though he didn't need the confirmation. "You come in here with that cock tease of a dress and you aren't wearing panties." Jealousy and desire twisted viciously through him. "Were you going to give Aaron a little show?"

"Oh, please. Give me a little credit." She lifted her chin. "I'm proving a point. You, Gideon Novak, don't get to make my decisions for me. I appreciate your help, but that's where it ends."

She didn't want him.

He was good enough to fuck but not good enough to listen to.

He kept a white-knuckled grip on his temper because having a knock-down, drag-out fight here and now wasn't an option for either of them. Not to mention the fact that he didn't have a *right* to be pissed. She'd laid out the terms that first day, and if he chose to ignore them, that was on him—not on Lucy.

It didn't make how shitty this situation was any easier to swallow.

Gideon stepped back. "The table. Bend over it."

Her eyebrows inched up. "You can't be serious."

"As a fucking heart attack. I told you what would happen if you showed up like that, and you were all too eager to pick up that gauntlet. Choices have consequences, Lucy. This is one of them."

She backed toward the table. One step. Two. "The consequences being that you'll spank my ass red and then fuck me right here."

She wants it.

It didn't soothe his temper. If anything, it ratcheted it up a notch. She might want *it* but she didn't want *him*. "The table."

Lucy turned and, prim as a princess, bent over the table. She seemed to consider and then lowered her chest farther until the top half of her body was flush against the polished wood. The position left her ass in the air and had her skirt riding up so he could *see* how turned on she was by this.

"Which part is getting you?" He stood between her and the door and pushed her dress the last few inches to bare her completely. "The spanking, the defiance, or the fact that we're in an unlocked room where anyone could walk in—including your fucking date?"

She tilted her ass up, just a little, an offer that made his mouth water. But it was her words that sealed her fate. "All of the above."

Fuck me.

He placed a steadying hand on the now-bare small of her back. "Brace yourself." Gideon wasn't into pain play, and he didn't think Lucy craved more than some rough-and-tumble shit, so he delivered a smack to her ass designed to sting without any lasting pain once they were through. Her gasp was almost a moan.

Gideon alternated smacks, giving each of her perfect fucking cheeks three. Enough to redden them as promised, but not more than that. He slipped a hand between her legs and groaned when he found her drenched. "You're going to fucking kill me."

He pulled out his wallet and retrieved the condom

he'd stashed there this morning. The crinkle of the wrapper sounded unnatural in the silence of the room, but he could barely hear it over the roaring in his ears. He nudged her legs wider and notched his cock at her entrance. "Next time, obey."

"Not likely." She used her forearm to muffle a moan when he shoved all the way into her.

Damn him to hell, but he loved that she pushed back. She'd been so timid in some ways their first couple of times together, and this defiance was more like the Lucy he used to know. He gripped her hips and pulled almost all the way out before he slammed back into her again. It was good—so fucking good—but it didn't satisfy the feral edge of rage he'd been riding for damn near twenty-four hours.

Gideon pulled out of her and flipped her around. She barely caught herself on his shoulders when he hooked the back of her thighs and lifted her onto the edge of the table. *Better.* But not enough. He yanked down her dress, baring her breasts. "Fucking *hell*, Lucy." He spread her legs wide and shoved into her, his gaze glued to the way her small breasts bounced with each thrust.

It wasn't enough to erase the image of her wearing that dress while chatting up Aaron.

Don't have a right to be jealous.

Don't give a damn if I have a right or not.

"Touch yourself. I want to feel you coming around my cock." He maintained his hold on her hips as she reached between her thighs and stroked her clit. Every thrust ground him against her fingers, the sensation as unbearably erotic as the sight of her touching herself while he fucked her.

Her body tightened around him and she cried out as she came. Gideon tried to hold out, but there was no fighting against the intoxication that was Lucy. He came with a curse. His breath tore from his lungs and he had to keep a death grip on the table to keep from hitting his knees.

It had never been like this for him before. He'd cared about women—even loved them—but the insanity Lucy drew out of him without seeming to try all that hard blew his fucking mind.

He stared into her bright blue eyes and wondered how the hell he was supposed to go back out into that club and pretend like he hadn't just been inside her.

As soon as she had control of her legs again, Lucy climbed off the table and fixed her dress. She could feel Gideon watching her, but she ignored him and pulled a pair of panties she'd stashed earlier out of her purse. She slipped them on and double-checked to make sure she wasn't in danger of indecent exposure. She straightened and froze. "What?"

"You just pulled panties out of your purse."

Heat flared over her exposed skin, but she forced herself to meet his gaze. "Yes, I did."

He didn't move, but he seemed closer. "I don't know whether to be impressed or pissed the fuck off. You baited me on purpose."

"Yes, I did," she repeated. "I was also proving a point. I won't allow you to control every aspect of these dates, but this thing between us is separate from that. For the duration, I'm yours." The words felt funny, as if she was declaring more than she intended, but she couldn't take them back without sounding ridiculous and giving them more weight than they deserved. *It's the truth. We're exclusive.*

But only sexually. There wasn't—couldn't—be anything more between them. She had her plan and Gideon hadn't held down a relationship for longer than two weeks the entire six years she'd known him. Even if Lucy was willing to bend on this—and she couldn't afford to be—Gideon would lose interest right around the time she needed him the most.

There would be no change of plans. They might fit better sexually than she could have dreamed, but that didn't mean anything in the grand scheme of things. She'd let good chemistry sideline her before—or what she'd *thought* was good chemistry. She wouldn't do it again, even if this felt as different from that as night to day.

"Mine for the duration." It sounded funny coming from him, too. Or maybe those were the butterflies erupting in her stomach.

She couldn't manage a smile, so she nodded. "Now, can we please go out there and meet this guy? Not to mention I haven't seen Roman in years and you hustled me past him so fast, I didn't even get to say hello." As ridiculous as it was, the thing she'd ended up missing most about being with Jeff was his friends.

Gideon had disappeared the second she'd broken up with Jeff and the rest of that group hadn't put up more than a token effort to keep in touch. To be fair, she hadn't tried, either. It was hard to look them in the face and know that they'd all had at least some idea of Jeff's extracurricular activities well before she had.

It doesn't matter anymore. I won't let *it matter.*

She didn't wait for Gideon to answer before she marched to the door and back the way they'd come. There was no helping her flushed cheeks, but she'd purposefully styled her hair a little wild in the event that Gideon was good on his threats. She might not be willing to admit it aloud—to him—but she was so very glad he had. The first two times with him had been wonderful beyond measure, but last night and tonight felt like the *real* Gideon. The man beneath the carefully controlled exterior.

She wanted more.

In fact, the last thing she wanted to do was exactly what she was doing—walking back into the VIP section. Much more enjoyable to slip out the back door with Gideon and go to one of their apartments to relieve the tension that only continued to rise the longer they were sleeping together.

It wasn't an option.

She ignored the way Roman glanced over her shoulder to where Gideon had no doubt just stepped into the room, speculation in his hazel eyes. Lucy gave him a big smile. "Roman, how have you been?"

"Well. Really well." He took her hand and stepped a little too close to be comfortable, his handsome face severe. She tensed and his next words did nothing to dispel the feeling. He kept his tone barely above a whisper. "I'm so sorry. If I'd have known he was going to be here, I would have passed on the information."

It took her pleasure-drugged brain several seconds to catch up. He wasn't talking about Aaron.

He was talking about Jeff.

She turned horror-movie slow toward the sound of a painfully familiar laugh. Jeff sat next to a pretty redhead and the entirety of his attention appeared to be on her. Lucy hadn't seen him in nearly two years—not since she'd thrown every single item he'd owned out their second-story apartment window—and she hated that he looked good. There was no extra weight, no puffy face that would indicate alcoholism, no slovenly appearance.

In fact, Jeff looked better than ever.

Lucy, no doubt, looked like she'd just been up to illicit activities in the back room—because she had been.

She looked up at Roman and didn't know what she was supposed to say or do. Jeff hadn't seen her yet, but it was just a matter of time before he did. She wasn't ready. She'd fought long and hard to get past the damage he'd done to her, but occupying the same space as him was enough to bring the truth flashing in front of her eyes.

She was still making her choices because of Jeff.

A hand pressed against the small of her back and Gideon's crisp scent wrapped around her. He stepped into view, blocking Jeff from her sight—or her from Jeff's. If Lucy felt off center, Gideon looked ready to shoot fire out of his eyes at Roman.

"Hey, man, like I just told Lucy—I didn't know he'd be here or I'd have let *you* know. He just showed up."

She pressed a hand to her chest. *I can't breathe.* An invisible band closed around her, tightening with each exhalation until black dots danced across her vision. Two years later and he still had so much power over her. She hated it. She hated *him*.

"Holy shit. Look what the cat dragged in." Jeff's voice came from directly behind Gideon.

Roman and Gideon looked at her, identical expressions on their faces. Asking how she wanted to handle this. If Lucy so much as blinked, she had a feeling Gideon would sweep her out of there without hesitation—and Roman would block Jeff from following if he tried.

But that was what she was so very tired of—letting Jeff's bullshit dictate how she handled any given situation.

Lucy lifted her chin, giving a slight nod. Gideon frowned, but he and Roman parted, taking up positions facing Jeff and only leaving a small sliver of a gap between them—standing sentry between her and her ex.

For all his pleased tone, Jeff's blue eyes were cold. The redhead on his arm didn't seem particularly happy, either, and Lucy spent a worthless few seconds wondering what he'd told her about this encounter. It didn't matter. *Jeff* didn't matter.

Or at least, he shouldn't.

She put all of her not inconsiderable willpower into appearing surprised. "Jeff. I had no idea you came here anymore."

"Not often." The look he shot the men in front of her was downright lethal.

Apparently his friendship with them hadn't lasted any longer than hers had. Lucy had known that about Gideon, but it comforted her to think of Jeff feeling just as abandoned as she had, even on that small scale.

He didn't jump in to say anything else, so she went with the first thing that popped into her mind. "You look well." *Meaningless chitchat.*

"I am well. Better than ever, really." His gaze jumped between her and Roman and Gideon. "You three look cozy." There was no mistaking the undertone of the statement. *Which one are you fucking?*

Looking too much into this. Get hold of yourself.

Gideon surprised her by taking a step back and pressing his hand to the small of her back. "We were just leaving."

At that, Jeff's mask slipped. His brows dropped, the first indication of what had always turned into a huge fight—one she had no chance of winning. Jeff seemed to take in her dress for the first time, his gaze leisurely raking over her body, pausing at her breasts and her bruised-feeling lips. "You and Gideon, huh? You took a pretty high-and-mighty stance with me when you broke off our engagement, and now you're fucking my best friend. Classy, Lucy, really classy."

No matter how much she told herself that his opinion didn't matter, it still felt like he'd sucker punched her. "It's not like that."

"It's exactly like that." Gideon spoke over her. He slipped his arm around her waist, pulling her against his side. "You fucked up and lost her. That's not on anyone but you, so don't start spouting that bullshit." He looked down at her, his expression hard. "You ready to go?"

"Please." She didn't want to stand there any longer than strictly necessary. The fact she hadn't sprinted for the exit was a win, as far as Lucy was concerned. Asking anything more of herself was out of the question.

Gideon nodded and glanced at Roman. "Next time."

"For sure."

He didn't give her a chance to say anything further before he steered them out of the VIP section and through to the front door. But what else was there to say? Anything she could come up with on that short walk sounded defensive, as if they'd done something wrong.

Well, I am *sleeping with him.*

But not dating him. Even if I was—it's been two years.

Two incredibly long and lonely years.

Lucy couldn't stop her shoulders from sagging the second they turned the corner away from the club. "That was terrible."

"I'm sorry, Lucy." His hand on her hip tensed, as if he wasn't sure whether he should pull her closer or release her. "I didn't know he'd show up. If I'd thought for a second it was a possibility, I wouldn't have taken you there."

"It's fine." It wasn't, but she should be stronger than this. Being brought to her knees emotionally just from running into her ex was inexcusably weak.

It wasn't even *Jeff* that was the problem. It was the fact that with one look, one carefully worded sentence, he could trigger every insecurity she fought so hard to banish. *He* wasn't the issue.

She was.

"It's not fine." Gideon stepped to the curb and flagged down a cab. "Your place or mine?"

If she let him, he'd talk through this with her. Gideon might be gloriously rough around the edges with a temper that would do a Viking proud, but he never failed to be careful around her.

Except when she pushed him hard enough that he forgot he was supposed to handle her with kid gloves.

There'd be no pushing him tonight. He'd pour her a glass of something alcoholic, sit her down and demand nothing but perfect honesty about how screwed up she was in her head. He'd pull out her issues and do his damnedest to fix them. Or, worse in some ways, he'd be wonderfully understanding and tell her it was okay.

She just…couldn't.

So incredibly weak.

Lucy didn't look at him as he pulled open the back door of the cab. "If it's all the same, I'd like to go home alone."

Gideon tensed and, out of the corner of her eye, she watched him fight an internal battle. Finally he shook his head. "If that's what you want."

It's not. "It is." Maybe if she got some distance, she could get her head on straight again. It was so hard to think with Gideon so close, his presence overwhelming her in every way. She couldn't handle it.

Lucy just needed time.

He stepped back, releasing her from her internal debate over whether she'd like him to force the issue or not. "Text me when you get back to your place."

"I will."

He waited until she slipped into the cab to say, "See you Saturday, Lucy."

CHAPTER TEN

GIDEON MADE IT until Wednesday. Three long-ass days in Seattle while he met with the first of the prospective fits he had for one of his clients. The guy was an advertising genius, though he was a little too free spirit for Gideon's straight-edged client. It might not be a deal-breaker, but it was something to take into account.

He shrugged out of his suit jacket and stared at his phone. Lucy hadn't called and she hadn't texted after the one letting him know that she was safely home. He had left New York with every intention of giving her the space she obviously wanted, but three days out of town had given him clarity.

She was running scared.

Seeing Jeff had screwed her up, and Gideon understood that. She hadn't wanted to further break herself open for *him*, and he respected that.

But she was closing him out.

He tossed his jacket on the bed and dialed her before he could think of all the reasons it was a bad idea. She hadn't brought him into this to work her shit out—she just wanted a husband and sex lessons. *Too damn bad. She signed up for* me*—and that's what she's going to get.*

"Lucy Baudin," she answered.

"Hey."

A long pause. "Hello, Gideon."

He hated the awkwardness seeping into this conversation before they'd exchanged half a dozen words. If he let it, it would become downright painful. Unacceptable. Gideon had never met a challenge he wasn't willing to go around, over or through, and a simple conversation wouldn't be the thing that stopped him in his tracks. "How's your week going?"

"Long, and it's only Wednesday. One of my clients is being difficult, and I'm having to work around her just to help her, which makes everything twice as challenging."

"You'll figure it out."

"I always do."

He dropped into the chair next to the desk. This wasn't working. Lucy held herself distant—polite—but there was none of the intimacy they'd started building. He hadn't even realized it was happening until that softness disappeared. *One way to put them back on solid ground.* "You home?"

"Yes. Hanging out with Garfunkel and wading through some old accounts for my current case—and drinking wine. This kind of investigating always requires wine."

"Naturally." He settled back into the chair and kicked off his shoes. "What are you wearing?"

Her surprised laugh was music to his ears. "Phone sex? Really, Gideon? Isn't that a bit juvenile?"

"We already had this discussion."

The amusement faded from her voice. "I suppose we did."

"On second thought, don't tell me what you're wearing. Show me. You by your computer?"

"Always."

"Give me two seconds." He grabbed his laptop and brought it online. A few button pushes later and he had a video call going through to Lucy.

She answered, looking unsure. "I guess I can hang up now."

"Yeah." He set down the phone and shifted to get comfortable. She looked good. She sat on her couch in the middle of several stacks of files, one housing her cat, and wore a fitted tank top and sleep shorts. Her shirt was thin enough that he could see the faintest outline of her nipples through the white fabric, and her sleep shorts gapped around her upper thighs in a way that made his mouth water. "Hey."

"Hey." She spoke just as softly. "Nice shirt."

"Thanks." He pulled his tie loose and tossed it onto the bed. "Have to look the part, though this guy isn't formal at all. He's a big fan of flannel, hair gel and skinny jeans."

She laughed softly. "Poor Gideon. You'd look downright fetching in flannel, but I like you without a beard. I'll hold out judgment on the skinny jeans, though they present some interesting possibilities."

His cock went rock-hard at the desire warming her

expression, but he kept his tone light. "I'll be sure to pick up something while I'm here."

"You don't have to."

"I know." But he wanted to show her that he valued her opinions. Gideon had never owned a piece of flannel clothing in his life, but if Lucy thought she'd like the look, he'd give it a shot. He noted the hesitance in her body language and refocused. "You always lounge in that sort of thing?" He waved to her clothing.

"This? Yes, I guess so." She shrugged. "It's comfortable."

"It's sexy as hell." He set his computer on the desk and leaned forward. "Let those thin little straps slide off your shoulders. I want to see you."

"Right now?" She looked around as if expecting him to jump out of a closet and tell her it was a joke. Lucy tucked a strand of her dark hair behind her ear. "I don't know if I'm ready for this."

She might very well not be, but if she didn't want to talk to him, then he'd keep them in the roles she'd set out for them. "Close your eyes." He waited for her to obey. "How do you feel when you take everything you think you *should* be feeling out of the equation?"

"Warm. Turned on." She hesitated. "A little intimidated. It's different when you're here with me, touching me. There's no room for being self-conscious."

"I've been thinking about you for five long-ass days and thinking about all the things I want to do to you when we're alone again."

"Things..." She licked her lips, one of her tells. Oh,

yeah, she liked this when she stopped remembering the reasons she shouldn't.

He kept going, pitching his voice low and intimate. "That lingerie shopping date we have? I've been thinking about sitting there and watching you come out of that room wearing one of those getups. Maybe you'll tease me, make me wait for it."

"Like this." She used a single finger to inch first one strap off her shoulder and then the other. The upper curve of her breasts caught the fitted fabric and he had to bite back a curse.

"Exactly like that. You know how bad I want it—want you—but I think you've got a little sadist in you because you like pushing my buttons. Making me crazy."

"I do." Her lips quirked up in a smile. "You're so controlled all the time. I like seeing what happens when the leash snaps."

He liked that she liked it. Gideon spent most of his days aware of how he presented himself and how everything from his tone to his appearance to his walk could be interpreted by clients and prospectives alike. He never let himself relax, because even in a social setting, there was no telling who was around.

There wasn't anyone around now—no one but him and Lucy.

"If I was there, I'd tug that top of yours a little lower. Yeah, like that." He watched, mouth dry, as she inched it down, stopping just below her nipples and then baring her breasts completely. "Exactly like that."

"This feels so dirty." She opened her eyes and pressed her lips together. "Would you…?"

"Tell me what you want and it's yours." He craved her words as much as he craved her touch. One was out of the question for the next few days—the other she gave him after the briefest hesitation.

"Unbutton your shirt." She leaned forward, the move making her breasts bounce a little. "I love your shoulders. Your suits have this way of masking how muscled they are, and seeing you shirtless makes me feel like it's my birthday."

He straightened so he could slip his shirt off and drop it on the floor. They stared at each other for a few seconds, Gideon drinking in the sight of her while she appeared to give him the same treatment. He spoke the second he saw doubt start creeping into her blue eyes. "Your breasts look like they ache. Palm them for me."

She instantly obeyed and then took it a step further and lightly pinched her nipples. This time he couldn't hold back his low curse. "Yeah, just like that."

"Are you…? Will you…?"

He instantly understood what she meant. "You want my cock?"

"Yes. Show me." She writhed a little, her hands moving with more purpose on her breasts.

He tilted his computer screen so the camera took in his lower half. He moved slowly, teasing her, and undid his slacks to withdraw his cock. He gave himself a long stroke and was rewarded with Lucy's moan. "You like that."

"I like that a lot."

"Take off your shorts. I want to see you stroking that pretty pussy until you come for me."

She barely hesitated this time before she released her breasts and lifted her hips to slide the shorts off.

He stroked himself again idly. "Spread your legs—yes, like that. Show me how you like it the same way you did that first time."

She slipped her hand between her thighs, parting her folds to draw a single finger over her clit. It was the single most devastating thing he'd ever seen.

Gideon watched avidly, taking in every detail and imprinting it into his memory. It was shitty not being able to be there and touch her, but it allowed him a perfect view and the distance to appreciate it in a new way.

Lucy was fucking magnificent.

After the first halting touches, she gave herself over to her pleasure—to both their pleasure—and stroked faster. Her head fell back against the couch and her body bowed as she pushed two fingers into her pussy. "I wish you were here."

"Saturday. I'll make it worth the wait."

"I don't know if anything is worth the wait." Her words were breathy and her breasts quivered with each exhalation. She managed to open her eyes. "I'm close, Gideon. Are you close?"

He'd been teetering on the edge the second she'd taken off her shorts, holding on through sheer force of will. "I'm close." He spoke through gritted teeth. Pressure built in his spine and his balls drew up, his cock swelling at the sight of her stroking herself to orgasm.

Lucy let her head hit the back of the couch again, but she kept her eyes open and on him as she fucked herself with her fingers. Her breath turned even choppier.

"Next time..." He had to stop and restart the sentence when she gasped. "Next time, you'll bring out that toy of yours. I want to see it sliding into you, vibrating and making you crazy."

"*You* make me crazy." Her back arched and every line of her body stood out as she came with his name on her lips.

Gideon couldn't hold on after that. He stroked faster, harder. She lifted her head in time to see him come in several spurts onto his stomach. He stared down at it marking his body and wondered when the hell his life had taken a hard right turn. A month ago he would have laughed someone out of the room for suggesting he'd be participating in a video call with mutual masturbation, let alone with Lucy Baudin.

And yet...here they were.

He reached down to grab his shirt and wipe himself off, and checked on her. Lucy had slid down to lie on the couch, and she watched him with a sleepy smile. "You've got that look on your face."

Her smile widened. "What look is that?"

"One that says you're thinking filthy thoughts." He liked that look. A lot.

She swept her hair off one shoulder and it pooled around her head on the cushion. "That's because I *am* thinking filthy thoughts." She bit her lip and then rushed on. "What time do you fly in Friday?"

"Our appointment is..." He stopped short. A slow tendril of pleasure that had nothing to do with sex rolled through him. "You want to see me Friday night."

"If that's okay. I know you'll be tired."

"It would take a whole hell of a lot more than a few hours' plane ride to make me too tired to see you. Though I don't fly in until after eleven."

She smiled. "I'll leave the key with the doorman."

Fuck yes. He damn well knew he was reading more into that choice than he should be, but it was hard not to. That simple sentence, more than anything else they'd done to this point, signaled her trust in him. "I'll stop by my place to drop my shit and then I'll be there."

"Perfect." She stretched. "Thank you for this, Gideon. All of it."

Strangely enough, he felt like *he* should be thanking *her.* He'd spent a long time just going through the motions and, for better or worse, Lucy had woken him up. He wanted to keep talking to her, but a quick glance at his phone showed that it was well past ten on the East Coast. "Don't let those files keep you up too late."

"I think I'm done for the night." She pulled on her shorts and resumed her comfortable-looking spot. "I had this really gorgeous guy call and talk me to orgasm just now, and I'm feeling all loose and relaxed, so I'm going to jump in the shower and head to bed to read for a bit. One of my favorite authors has a book out and I've been dying to start it."

I wish I was there. He didn't say it again. It was one thing to put those words out there when talking about sex—it was entirely another to do it now that the desire had cooled.

It was the truth, though.

He wanted to be there to pull her into a relaxing shower, to exchange small talk about nothing important while they got ready for bed, to settle in while she read her book and he finished answering the last few emails of the day. Gideon wanted it so bad, he could barely breathe past the need.

He couldn't say any of that now without scaring the shit out of Lucy.

But he managed a smile. "You'll have to tell me about it when I see you."

Lucy gave him a strange look. "You want to hear about my book?"

"Sure." If only because it was something she was interested in and obviously passionate about—and had been for as long as he'd known her, though she used to hide them under a pillow when he and Jeff would walk into the room. Jeff had always made snide comments that he covered up as joking, and Gideon should have paid more attention to Lucy's reaction to those comments. He'd known his friend was a jackass, but he hadn't realized the depth of the damage Jeff was dealing her.

"That's nice of you to say, but we really don't have to talk about my romance novel addiction."

Damn it, she was doing it again. He leaned forward until his face filled the video screen. "I wouldn't ask if I didn't want to know. Nothing but honesty between us, remember? It interests you, so I want to know more. It's as simple as that."

She opened her mouth, seemed to reconsider arguing with him and shut it. "That makes sense."

"Because it's the truth." He stomped down on his anger. Hard. It wasn't directed at Lucy, and it wasn't fair to take his fury at himself and Jeff out on *her*. Gideon kept his tone low and even. "Enjoy the rest of your night, Lucy."

"You, too." She looked away and then back at the camera. "If you change your mind about Friday, I'll understand."

God, she was fucking killing him. "I'll see you Friday night."

CHAPTER ELEVEN

LUCY HAD EVERY intention of staying awake to greet Gideon. If nothing else, she was sure nerves would keep her alert until he arrived. She hadn't counted on the long day.

It had started at 5:00 a.m. when she'd gotten a call from the office that there was a new client on retainer and that Lucy was needed at the woman's home immediately. Things had only gone downhill from there. The client—accused of money laundering—was as high maintenance as they came, so Lucy'd had her work cut out for her.

Throw in the partners dragging her into a boardroom for a progress report the second she'd set foot in the office, and she was exhausted. Her other clients couldn't be shoved to the back burner, no matter how important the new one was, so she'd worked late to ensure she was ready for court on Monday.

All of it had added up to an exhaustion she couldn't fight, no matter how entertaining the newest episode of her favorite medical drama. Her blinks became longer and longer, and the next thing she knew, she roused to the feeling of strong hands sliding up her thighs.

That alone should have scared the crap out of her, but Gideon's scent wrapped around her, setting her at ease even before she was fully awake. She blinked down at him as he hooked his arms beneath her and lifted her off the couch. "I can walk."

"Humor me." He strode down her hallway without turning on any lights and toed open the door to her bedroom. She hadn't bothered leaving lights on in her room and Lucy regretted that when Gideon set her on the bed and stripped in quick, efficient movements. She moved to do the same, but he beat her there, carefully pulling her oversize T-shirt off. Since Lucy had been expecting him, she hadn't worn anything else.

His quick intake of breath was a reward in and of itself. She ran her hand up his chest. "Hey."

"Hey." He guided her to lie on the bed, quickly put on a condom and covered her with his body. "You looked comfortable on the couch."

"I was." She wrapped her legs around his waist and arched up to kiss his throat. "This is better."

"Agreed." He laced his fingers through her hair and guided her mouth to his, kissing her lazily, as if he had no idea of the need already building in her core. Need that only Gideon seemed to be able to sate. He took his time reacquainting himself with her mouth before he moved to her neck and collarbone. "I was going to wake you up in a very specific way."

"Mmm." She reached between them to stroke him.

"This is better." She notched his cock at her entrance. "I need you."

He slid into her in a single move and kissed her again with them sealed as closely as two people could be. Pressure built between them, but his big body kept Lucy pinned in place so she couldn't do anything more than shake. Even that tiny movement ratcheted up her desire until she couldn't stop a whimper of need from escaping. "Gideon, stop teasing me."

"I know I'm not supposed to say it, but I missed the fuck out of you this week."

Her breath got tangled somewhere between her lungs and throat. The words she was supposed to say lingered on the wrong side of her lips. *That's not what we are.* It might be the correct thing to say, but it wasn't the *right* thing to say—or the truth. "I missed you, too."

He finally moved, rocking against her. It wasn't enough, but that made it all the hotter. She did her best to arch, fighting against the weight of his body and loving every second of it. "More."

"Demanding," he murmured against her lips. "I waited seven fucking days to be inside you again, and I'm going to take my time and enjoy it." He dragged his mouth down her throat, his whiskers rasping against her sensitized skin. "I like having you like this."

"Furious?"

He chuckled, the low sound vibrating through her. "Needy. Wanting. As close as you'll ever come to begging."

"Would begging make a difference?"

His lips brushed the shell of her ear. "No."

Lucy shivered, her breath releasing in a sob. It felt too good and she needed more. But he was right—she loved every second of this. Their bodies slicked with sweat as he kept up those slight rocking movements, every single one inching her closer to oblivion. His pelvis created delicious friction against her clit, and she found herself talking without having any intention of doing so. "That feels so good, Gideon. Don't stop. Never stop." She dug her fingers into his ass, loving the way he growled against her neck. "I love this."

"I know." He slipped one arm beneath the small of her back and the other up her spine to cup her head. She'd thought they were as close as two people could be. He proved her wrong. Lucy slid her feet down to hook around his calves, grinding against him. Gideon kissed her as if he couldn't help himself. His tongue stroked hers, plunging deep, the way she wanted him to elsewhere. Right when she caught his rhythm, he withdrew and then stroked deep again, starting the process over. It made her crazy—crazier.

He knew. He always seemed to know exactly how close to the edge she was.

Gideon began to move. His hips mirrored the movements his tongue had made, stroking deep and then withdrawing before slamming home again.

Lucy couldn't think, couldn't move, couldn't even breathe. Her entire existence boiled down to the places Gideon touched her and his cock between her thighs. Pressure wound tighter and tighter, turning her into a wild creature with no thought but her own pending orgasm.

It hit her like a freight train and she let loose a keening cry that didn't sound human to her ears. Lucy couldn't do more than cling to Gideon as his strokes became more and more ragged and rough until he orgasmed with a curse. He dropped slightly to the side of her, but shifted to pull her leg up and over his hip, keeping them close.

She tried to get her racing heart under control. "That was some wake-up."

"It's good to see you, Lucy." Such a polite thing to say considering their current position.

I think I prefer hearing that you missed me.

With the post-orgasm bliss numbing her common sense, she couldn't quite shut that thought down. She crossed the line they'd drawn in the sand. "Stay."

"What?"

She ran her hand up his arm. "Stay. It's almost morning and there's no point in you cabbing back to your place and turning around to do it again in a few hours. Just…stay here with me."

"You sure that's what you want?" There wasn't a single thing in his voice to indicate what *he* wanted.

"Yes. If you want to, of course." *Maybe I misheard him and I'm wrong about this entire situation.*

Gideon delivered a devastating kiss and climbed off the bed. "Give me a few."

"Sure." She waited for him to walk into her bathroom and shut the door before she relaxed and sighed, staring at the ceiling. *What am I doing?*

He was back before she could muster the energy to second-guess herself. Gideon pulled down the comforter and waited for her to climb beneath it before he followed suit. She tensed, waiting for the inevitable awkwardness, but he just slipped in behind her and guided her so he could spoon her. He kissed the back of her neck. "Sleep."

Lucy thought it impossible, but the heat of him and the feel of safety being tucked against his big body lulled her circling thoughts to a standstill. Between one breath and the next, she slipped into a deep sleep.

Gideon woke to the smell of bacon. For one disorientating moment he didn't know where he was, but then the events of the night came rushing back to him. Lucy. Her apartment. Sleeping here. He sat up and scrubbed a hand over his face. *I told her I missed her and then I stayed the night.* For all his intentions of respecting *her* intentions, Gideon was doing a piss-poor job of following through.

Worse, he'd been so focused on himself, he hadn't stopped to ask her how she was doing after seeing Jeff again—a week ago. *Fuck me.* He stopped in the bathroom to brush his teeth as best he could with a finger and pulled on his pants.

He found Lucy in the kitchen, opening a series of take-out containers. She looked fresh and happy, her hair back in a low-key ponytail, and wore black leggings and a blue sweater that matched her eyes. She smiled when she saw him. "Morning."

"Morning." He took in the spread. "What's all this?"

"I think we can both agree that cooking isn't one of my strengths, so I popped out and grabbed something edible." She grabbed two mugs from one of her cabinets. "Coffee, however, I am capable of throwing together."

"Survival skill."

"Exactly." She passed him a full cup and her expression turned serious. "Can we have today?"

Gideon took a careful drink of the scalding liquid and contemplated her. For all that she appeared relaxed on the surface, there was an underlying tension there. "And after today?"

"I figure we're due a conversation, but we have plans today and I don't want to ruin them by talking this to death. I'm happy and I want to hold on to that."

Meaning that this talk wouldn't make her feel happy—or him, for that matter. Gideon already knew what was coming. He'd muddied the waters by showing up last night, and taken it a step further by staying and holding her while they'd slept. They hadn't talked about lessons after that first time they'd had sex, which was supposed to be the whole purpose of this exercise. She'd also been on exactly one date.

He had to fix that.

He would rather chew off his own arm than set her up on any more dates, but that was what he'd given his word he'd do. Lucy trusted him and he couldn't betray that trust. *Not again.*

Gideon forced an easy smile onto his face. "Sure, we can have today." He didn't want to have that talk any more than she appeared to want it, so he wasn't going to worry about a few hours spent without overthinking things. "I thought you had lunch with your sister?"

"She got called in to cover a class and had to cancel." Lucy gave him a small smile. "I know we had planned for this afternoon, but I'm free all day if you are."

"I'm free." Gideon had been looking forward to this date all damn week, so he hadn't put anything else on his schedule.

Because that was exactly what this was, even if Lucy didn't realize it. A date.

Maybe she does realize it and that's why she's asking to shelve the conversation we obviously need to have until tonight.

She gave him a sunny smile. "Good. In that case, eat up while I jump in the shower." She pushed the food toward him, grabbed her mug and strolled out of the kitchen.

He spent half a second considering following her and making the shower one to remember, but if Gideon read the signs correctly, Lucy needed time. It had been that way with them from the start of this—she'd take a step forward and need time to acclimate. He could respect that. He *would* respect that. If he pushed too hard, too fast, she'd bolt, and this time he'd never hear from her again. It wasn't a risk he was willing to take, especially now when it felt like they were close to something that could actually be real.

If she'd take that leap of faith with him.

He ate quickly and cleaned up the containers. By

that time, the shower had turned off, so Gideon grabbed the bag he'd brought in the night before and hauled it into her room.

Lucy glanced over from where she'd just walked through the bathroom door. She had a fluffy towel wrapped around her, and though it hid her curves, the exposed skin of her shoulders and calves had him craving the feel of her. She narrowed her eyes. "You didn't go home last night, did you?"

There was no use in denying it. "Nope." He'd wanted to see her—had *needed* to see her—and the extra forty minutes it would have taken were forty minutes too many. He nodded at the bathroom door. "Mind if I use your shower?"

"Of course not. Go for it."

He didn't need to be told twice. Gideon showered quickly, pausing long enough to wish he had time to shave, but he wasn't likely to see anyone he knew professionally today. He paused in front of his suitcase. Lucy had been wearing casual clothes earlier, and it might make her uncomfortable if he used his last suit. The other option wasn't as comfortable for *him*, but he'd make do.

He had promised her, after all.

When he walked out of the bathroom, she froze. "You…" She gave herself a shake. "Sorry, I don't think I've ever seen you rumpled-looking before—not even in college."

He glanced down at his designer jeans and the flannel shirt he'd thrown over a white T-shirt. "I'm not rumpled."

"You are most definitely rumpled." She moved closer, taking him in as a small smile pulled at the edges of her lips. "You look like you should be standing on a porch on some mountainside, a steaming cup of coffee in hand while you contemplate whatever it is that lumberjacks contemplate." She ran her hands up his chest and over his shoulders. "I like it."

"Rumpled suits me."

"You don't have to sound so cranky when you say it." She smoothed down his shirt, actually leaning forward a few inches before she seemed to remember herself and took several steps back. "I'm ready when you are."

She wore a different variation of what she'd had on earlier: dark leggings, a long black T-shirt and a slouchy knitted cardigan thing. Her pants were tucked into a sleek pair of knee-high boots. *Rumpled* was not a word he'd use to describe her, but with her hair falling in careless waves to her shoulders, she looked relaxed. Almost peaceful.

He liked it.

Gideon pulled on his shoes and then they headed down to the street. Lucy paused on the sidewalk. "It's such a nice day."

He could pick up a clue as obvious as that one. "We could walk. It's only a handful of blocks."

"Are you sure? We didn't really talk about what your other plans are for the day and—"

"There are no other plans." He cut in before she could talk herself out of the whole day. "I worked all week. I cleared today for you, Lucy."

"Oh. Well…oh." She managed to look everywhere but at him. "I'm sorry—is this weird? It didn't feel all that strange when I suggested it earlier, but I think common sense has taken hold."

"More like nerves." He pressed his hand to the small of her back. "Walk with me, Lucy. What's the harm that could come of it?"

CHAPTER TWELVE

What's the harm that could come of it?

Lucy forced herself to look at Gideon. His expression was as open as she'd ever seen it, inviting her to take this first step with him. First step into *what*, though? It had been an off-the-cuff thing to tell him that she wanted today, but through her shower and then his, the importance of that statement—this plan—had grown to epic proportions.

It felt like a date.

Except she wasn't supposed to be dating Gideon. She was supposed to be dating the men Gideon set her up with.

He didn't look particularly concerned that they had left the boundary of their agreed-upon relationship in the rearview. He offered his arm, the old-world gesture so very Gideon.

She slipped her hand onto his arm and fell into step with him as if it was the most natural thing in the world. Maybe it was. She didn't know anymore. These days, it felt like up was down and down was up, and Lucy was bouncing somewhere in the middle.

"How was your trip? Other than having to fend off a city full of free spirits." She injected false sympathy into her tone. "You poor thing."

Gideon shook his head. "You mock me while you were here, safe in New York. The people on that coast aren't anything like *our* people. They chat." He gave a mock shudder. "You wouldn't last two days."

"On the contrary, I'm not nearly as cranky and anti-social as you are. I'd be fine."

"There is that." He pulled her to a stop at the curb as cars whizzed past. "It was a productive trip. One of my prospective fits looks like she'll work out, and I managed to source a secondary backup in Portland. Those two cities are filled to the brim with tech geniuses, so if I can lure either woman over here, they'll have jobs waiting."

A barb of something like jealousy embedded itself in Lucy's throat. He'd spent a full week in endless meetings between Seattle and Portland, and a few of the people he'd met with had been women. It shouldn't matter. Lucy had no claim on Gideon. Not really. They might be exclusive for the time being, but there was a looming expiration date. He could have plans to hook up with one of those women—or both—and Lucy didn't have the right to be upset about it.

That didn't change the fact that her chest ached at the very thought.

"Maisey Graham has been married to her high school sweetheart since the month after graduation, and he owns his own business, so relocation isn't out of the question." Gideon spoke low enough that she had to lean in to hear his words, very carefully not looking at him. "Jericha Hurley will be eighteen in two months, though she's damn near a certified genius and she's got her pick of companies vying for her attention."

He knew.

The ache in her chest got worse. She managed to breathe past it—barely. "It's none of my business."

"Honesty, Lucy."

She didn't want to be honest. She wanted to shove her head in the sand. They crossed the road and kept going down the block. She tried to pinpoint exactly what the problem was. *Easy enough—I'm jealous of the thought of Gideon spending time with other women.* Not just spending time, though. Having long meetings, likely alone, on the other side of the country. "It's not that I think you'd do that after you told me we were exclusive."

"The fear is there all the same." He set his free hand over hers and squeezed. "That's not something you just get over."

Maybe she would have. If she'd put half the effort into dating that she'd put into her career, she'd have worked through what was apparently a hair trigger. *Or maybe it wouldn't have mattered.* There was no way to tell, and it was a moot point. "We have to fix this."

"What?"

"This is another issue. I can't very well marry someone if the thought of them being alone in a room with a woman is going to send me into a jealous spiral. They're all businessmen, and so that sort of thing will pop up. There's no avoiding it." She latched on to the idea, turning it over in her mind. "We can start at the lingerie shop."

Gideon pulled them out of the path of foot traffic and guided her to the brick wall of a nearby storefront. He let go and took her by the shoulders. "Lucy, stop."

"Don't take that tone with me. I'm not being crazy."

"Everything about this situation is crazy. No, don't get your back up. It is and you know it, and I'm here willingly, taking part in it." He looked like he wanted to shake some sense into her. "You're asking me to… What? Flirt with someone in front of you? More?"

More?

Her entire body clenched as if trying to reject the very idea of Gideon doing *more* with someone else. *I am out of control.* "If that's what it takes."

A muscle jumped in his jaw. "No."

"Excuse me?"

He shook his head. "Absolutely not. You pick one of these assholes and he flirts with another woman in front of you—or at all—and you get out, Lucy. You hear me? That is not normal, and no man who respects his partner would put them in that situation where they have to wonder if something more is going on. I would never so much as look at another woman if I was with you—in your presence or not."

"But—"

"But nothing. There are a lot of gray areas in relationships. This isn't one of them. Short of there being extenuating circumstances that are agreed upon by both parties, there is a clear line and no one should be crossing it."

She stared. This was supposed to be all in theory—a test run of sorts—but Gideon spoke like it was a personal attack on him. *Because it is.* She didn't know what to do, so she slipped her arms around his waist and pulled him in for a hug. "I'm sorry."

He cursed, but he wrapped his arms around her. "You have nothing to be sorry for."

"I'm blurring the lines." She wasn't even sure where the lines were at this point. Having sex was one thing, though they hadn't even done *that* right because she was too busy enjoying herself to pay attention to whatever he tried to teach her. On what was supposed to be her second date, she was more excited about pushing Gideon's buttons than she was about meeting her actual date.

And now she was getting jealous.

He pulled her tighter against him. "We'll talk about it tonight." He stepped back and reclaimed her hand. "Come on."

Lucy didn't know whether to look forward to the conversation or to dread it. When she'd initially brought it up, she'd deluded herself with the falsity that she had everything under control. Twenty minutes into this day and she'd proved herself wrong half a dozen times. Gideon was probably going to sit her down and explain how out of line she'd been lately.

Let it go. You can obsess about every word and touch and meaning once he's left tonight.

Strangely enough, that made her feel better. Or

maybe it was his fingers laced through hers as they walked down the street. Two blocks later, he pulled her to a stop in front of a boutique lingerie shop. "Yes?"

She took in the window display, a perfect blend of tasteful and risqué. The mannequins reclined on a lounging sofa, both wearing jewel-toned bustiers, ruffled boy-short panties, with garters and thigh-highs. One had on a lace shrug that looked like something out of an old black-and-white movie. "Yes."

She couldn't wait to get into that dressing room with Gideon.

One minute Gideon was leading Lucy into the lingerie boutique, the next, a whirlwind of a saleswoman had stationed him in one of the private change areas and led Lucy away. He blinked at the opening leading into the rest of the store but didn't move from his assigned spot. *That was smoothly done.*

Content to leave Lucy at the mercy of the woman, he surveyed the changing area. It was a clever design, each of the three doorways leading to a small sitting area and an individual change room. The whole setup created the feeling of an intimate environment for shopping for the most intimate of clothing. He approved.

Gideon hadn't decided whether now was the time to play on Lucy's fantasy of change room sex. He'd intended it initially, but their conversation on the walk over had put things up in the air. He'd already pressed her hard just by staying last night. Her showing signs of jealousy was a sign that she felt more than just sexual attraction, but it obviously set her off balance and made her uncomfortable.

He sat back and scrubbed a hand over his face. The truth was, he didn't know how to play this. He'd made his career on being able to read people and find good fits, but he was fumbling around in the dark when it came to Lucy. He felt like he was back in high school, trying to express interest without hanging himself out to dry and becoming the laughingstock of the school.

Except the stakes were a whole hell of a lot higher now.

The saleswoman had hustled Lucy into the change room so fast, he hadn't seen more than a flash of bright colors attached to hangers before the door shut. The saleswoman—a little Goth woman who stood five feet tall, if that—emerged a few seconds later. She had purple streaks in her black hair and a lip ring. She winked at him and raised her voice. "You let me know if you need any different sizes or want to try something else. There's a button in there that will ding me, but otherwise, I'll leave you to it."

"Thank you." Lucy's voice was muffled.

The saleswoman stopped next to him. "Special lady you have there."

"Yes." She wasn't telling him anything he didn't know. She lingered for a second, something obviously on her mind, but he didn't have the patience to deal with it when he could hear the slide of cloth against skin in the dressing room. "Thank you."

"Let me know if you need anything. We have coffee and water." She waited half a beat and then was gone, striding out the door and into the main boutique.

Gideon drummed his fingers on his knee and waited.

Then waited some more.

Five minutes later his frayed patience gave out. He rose and stalked to the dressing room door. "Lucy."

"Yes?" She sounded small and unsure.

"Do you need assistance?"

"No."

He stared at the door, willing her to open it. She didn't. Gideon sighed. "Is there a problem?"

"No. Yes. I don't know. I just feel absolutely ridiculous."

He considered and discarded several responses to that. None of them was worth the breath it would take to give them voice. "Open the door."

"It's fine, Gideon. This was a silly idea. Just give me a minute to change back into my clothes and we can find something else to do today."

"Open the door," he repeated.

Her bare feet padded over the tiled floor and he held his breath as they approached the door. And then it was open and a vision from every one of his fantasies stood in front of him. Lucy wore nude-colored thigh-highs, held up by an emerald garter belt. Its decorative lace almost hid the fact that her panties barely hid anything at all. And the bustier was a work of art, offering her breasts with peekaboo lace that showcased her nipples apparently by accident. The whole thing was a goddamn tease and he loved it. "You look ravishing."

She put her hands on her hips, at her sides, and then finally crossed them over her chest. "*Ravishing* is a strong word."

"It fits." He stepped into the dressing room and shut the door behind him, unable to take his eyes off her. "If you don't like it, *divine*, *exquisite* and *breathtaking* are also accurate."

Her eyebrows inched up. "Do you have a thesaurus tucked into your back pocket?"

"Don't need one." He stopped in front of her and uncrossed her arms so he could see her. As with all things Lucy, both she and the lingerie were even better up close. Gideon stroked his hands down her sides and ran his thumb over the garter belt. What he found had him going to his knees in front of her. "Your panties are on top."

"Well, yes." A blush spread over her pale cheeks and down her chest. "I'd already decided to buy it based on the color, so I wanted the full effect."

There was only one reason to wear panties over the garter belt; they could be removed while leaving the rest of the lingerie on.

Gideon hooked the side of the thong with his thumbs and looked up her body to her face. "Yes?"

"Yes." The word was barely more than a stirring of the air between them.

He slid her panties down her legs, taking his time. "I'm buying this for you. Don't argue. This isn't a disagreement that you'll win."

"This getup is incredibly expensive." As he crouched, she lifted first one foot and then the other so he could remove the thong completely.

"Worth every penny." The garter belt framed her pussy to perfection, an offering he couldn't have resisted if he'd tried—and Gideon wasn't interested in trying. He guided one of her legs over his shoulder, a position that left her completely at his mercy. "Just a taste."

CHAPTER THIRTEEN

AT THE FIRST stroke of Gideon's tongue, Lucy forgot all the reasons this was a questionable idea. She didn't care. The only thing that mattered was his tongue lazily circling her clit. As if he had all the time in the world and they weren't in a public place.

A public place where every moan and sound could be heard by someone on the other side of the dressing room door.

She shivered, heat cascading through her body at the thought of someone listening. Someone knowing what they were doing. Someone thinking Gideon was so turned on by the lingerie that he couldn't wait for the time it'd take them to get home.

He'd had to have her right then and there.

His dark gaze met hers as he licked her again. "What are you thinking?"

She was thinking she wanted more. To be dirty. To break the rules.

Lucy reached down and tugged on his shoulders. Without saying another word, Gideon rose and let her guide him to sit on the bench that ran along the wall in the changing room. He watched her through hooded eyes as she undid the front of his jeans and climbed onto his lap. After a quick detour to her purse for a condom, she rolled it onto his length. He opened his mouth but Lucy pressed a single finger to his lips.

His eyes flashed in understanding and his lazy grin made her pussy clench. Lucy guided him inside her and sealed them together. She leaned forward until her lips brushed his ear. "Someone could hear."

"Yes." The word was barely more than a whisper. He reached up and pulled her bustier down to bare her breasts. "Hope you locked the door. She knocks on it and it'll swing right open. Give the woman the sight of a lifetime."

Her nipples tightened at the image his low words painted. It didn't matter that she knew for a fact the door was locked. It *could* be unlocked. Lucy held on to Gideon's shoulders and started to move. Each time she lifted almost all the way off his cock, her breasts brushed against his mouth and he kissed first one and then the other.

Thrust. Kiss. Thrust.

"Look at how beautiful you are." He gripped her chin and turned her face to the full-length mirror.

What a picture they made. Him fully clothed except for his cock disappearing and reappearing between her legs. Her mostly naked and riding him, her pale skin flushed with desire. Lucy couldn't take her gaze away from where one of his big hands held her hip while the other maintained its grip on her chin, to the look on his face as he stared at her in the mirror. She licked her lips. "*We* are beautiful."

He guided her back to face him. "Fuck me. Come on my cock. But be quiet or Agnes will hear."

The words unleashed the orgasm that had been building from the moment he'd slipped off her panties. Lucy buried her face in his neck and tried to muffle her cry as she came. Gideon looped an arm around her waist and lifted her to reverse their positions, sitting her on the bench with him kneeling between her thighs, his cock still buried inside her.

He held her thighs wide and proceeded to fuck her. She had to cling to the edge of the bench to keep from smacking against the wall with the strength of his thrusts. Through it all, his dark eyes swallowed her up, so full of things she couldn't put a name to. An expression almost like pain flickered over his face as he came with a muffled curse, hips still thrusting as if he never wanted to stop.

Lucy slumped back onto the bench and blinked at the reflection of herself. Gideon crouched in front of her, his dark eyes wild. He started to reach for her and stopped. "Your place. Now."

"We could..." She trailed off. *My place.* Despite the outstanding and filthy sex, she wanted more. She wanted skin on skin and Gideon's taste in her mouth. She wanted it all.

She nodded. "My place." She lifted her shaking hands to finish undoing her bustier, but Gideon beat her there. He undid the tiny clasps carefully, the delicate lace looking strange against his massive hands.

He slid it off her arms and folded it neatly on the bench next to her before giving the garter belt and stockings the same treatment. The panties finished off the pile.

He ran his hands up her legs. Lucy held her breath and arched her back a little. His pupils dilated, which was a reward in and of itself, but Gideon stood. "Get dressed." Then he was gone, snatching the lingerie off the bench and striding out the door, careful to not let it open too much.

She stared after him for a long moment before she dredged up the ambition to move. It was just as well he'd shown a little restraint or she had a feeling they wouldn't have left this dressing room for several hours. She wasn't sure if she was disappointed that he'd walked out or excited for what was to come.

Excited. Definitely excited.

She dressed quickly and paused to check her appearance in the mirror. Flushed cheeks, slightly wild eyes, skin a little too glowy. It was a good look, but there was no mistaking that she and Gideon had been up to no good behind the closed door. It was becoming a habit of theirs, though Lucy couldn't say she was sad about it. She liked the thrill of knowing there were people within hearing distance.

She liked that she was experiencing it with Gideon even more.

Lucy stopped short.

There it was. The thing she'd been doing her best not to think too hard about since their first time—since *before* their first time, if she was being honest. There'd always been an attraction simmering between her and Gideon, even when she'd been with Jeff. She'd gone out of her way to ensure she'd never given him any sign of it, because she'd been in a relationship.

Because she cared about Gideon as a friend, and if something had happened between them, she'd lose him.

There was no Jeff standing between them now, and her feelings for Gideon were significantly more complicated. There was lust, definitely. Her body craved his like she'd never craved anything—anyone—before.

But there were…feelings.

She gave herself a shake. It didn't matter if there were feelings or not. She'd set out the terms and Gideon had agreed to them. Changing the rules without notice meant she really *would* lose him and she hadn't come all this way to falter now. She'd missed him terribly these last couple of years, and the thought of going back to her life without him in it felt like she had a gaping hole in her chest.

Gideon wasn't the keeping kind. A lot had changed, but she couldn't afford to believe *that* had. He'd settle down someday, with the right woman, but he wasn't there yet. Even if he tried to give them a shot for her sake, it would self-destruct sooner rather than later.

No matter which way she looked at the situation, the end result was the same—if she changed the rules now, she would lose him. If she saw her original plan through to the end, she retained the chance to keep Gideon in her life.

Lucy would fight for that, even if it meant hurting herself to do so.

She took a deep breath and straightened her shoulders. *I can do this.* Lucy opened the change room door and marched out. Gideon stood by the entrance to the boutique and she headed his way, very carefully not looking for Agnes. They might be the only people in the shop, but they'd been in that room far too long to be doing anything but exactly what they'd been doing. *Focus, Lucy.* She licked her lips as she stopped next to Gideon. "My place?"

"I changed my mind."

She braced herself. "Oh?"

"That meal might have been sweet, but it won't sustain us for what I have in mind for later." He gave her a wolfish grin that had her warming even as she tried not to read into his words too much.

It won't sustain us.

He didn't mean anything by it—of that, Lucy was sure—but it served as yet another reminder that this was temporary and any effort to make it permanent would backfire spectacularly. She put on her best smile. "What's the plan, then?"

Gideon's grin dropped away and he studied her for a long moment, seeming to see through her façade. Finally he nodded, almost to himself. "Lunch. Then we'll head back to your place to finish what we started."

Not a brush-off, then, but a detour. She kept her shoulders from sagging through sheer stubbornness. "I could eat."

"Good." He touched the small of her back and ushered her out of the building. He didn't say anything as they walked down the street, and she was too twisted up inside her own head to try for conversation. Nothing she said right now would change the truth, and the weight of it threatened to send her scurrying back to her place to barricade herself in with Garfunkel and the work files she still had to find time for this weekend.

Their destination was a little restaurant on the second floor of a converted apartment building. They'd left most of the interior walls up and designed low lighting so that even in the middle of the afternoon, it gave the illusion of a night tucked away. The hostess led them to a room that might have been a closet at one point, though it had two doorways now and space for a little booth for two.

Gideon waited for her to slide in and then took the spot next to her. The hostess left and Lucy became aware of a low jazz song playing in the background. She ran her finger over the rough tabletop. "I didn't even know this place existed."

"It's new. A friend of mine bought the building a couple years back and construction just wrapped up a few months ago. The bottom floor is split into a clothing boutique and shoe store, and the third floor is privately owned."

She'd definitely come down here to check out the shoe store in the future. She twisted to face him, but he spoke before she could. "What happened back there?"

"Excuse me?"

"You know exactly what I'm talking about. You

were fine in the dressing room, and when you walked out, you'd put a wall up between us."

She desperately didn't want to talk about this, but his jaw was set in an all-too-familiar way. There would be no getting out of this conversation, short of crawling over the table and making a run for it. Since that was beneath Lucy's dignity—and she didn't know for certain that Gideon wouldn't just chase her down—she sighed. "We have clear boundaries."

"Mmm-hmm."

That response gave her no indication of what he thought of that, so she hedged. "Very clear boundaries."

Gideon drummed his fingers on the table. "Is the problem that you feel that I'm threatening the boundaries or that the boundaries themselves are the problem?"

Trust the man to just lay it out there with no qualms. She fought not to fidget. "I value our friendship. I know it may not seem like that after not speaking for two years, but I missed you terribly during that time and I feel like we're almost starting to reclaim that lost ground."

The guarded look on his face cleared. "You don't want to jeopardize our friendship."

"Exactly." She didn't mention the theoretical pending marriage or what their friendship might look like once she'd picked a man and followed through on that. The marriage might have sex included in the bargain, but it would still be a marriage without love. Having

Gideon in her life, even on the outskirts, wasn't something she was willing to give up.

Not now that she'd just gotten him back.

The waiter brought their waters and took their drink orders. Once the man disappeared through the doorway, Gideon turned back to her. "That gap in communication was as much my fault as it was yours. I let guilt get the better of me and figured that you didn't want to see my face any more than you wanted to see Jeff's."

"You...weren't wrong—at least, not at first." She'd been so hurt and angry and embarrassed that she hadn't wanted to see *anyone* for months after she'd broken off her engagement. The only person who'd ignored that was Becka, and even she'd had to come to Lucy. If Gideon had tried during that time, she would have slammed the door in his face.

By the time she'd gathered the strength to get back out into the world again, it was to find that her former friends had moved on without her. It made sense, in a way. She'd lost most of her good friends when she and Jeff had started dating—a sign she should have paid more attention to. He hadn't missed a beat after their breakup, and most of their friends had been his first, so they'd moved along with him.

It was Gideon's steady presence that she'd missed the most, but she hadn't known how to reach out to him.

Or if she even should.

I'm here now. We *are here now.*

She held herself steady. "Regardless, I feel like I just found you again."

"And you don't want to lose that." He said it almost as if musing to himself. When she tensed, he leaned back and slung an arm over the back of the booth. "I don't want to lose it, either, Lucy. I missed you, too. I'm still missing you, if we're going to be perfectly honest."

Her jaw dropped. "What are you talking about? I'm right here."

"Yes, you are." He pulled her closer, tucking her against his body. "But we haven't stopped to have a real conversation since you sat me down in your office and told me you wanted me to help you find a husband."

Lucy opened her mouth to say he was wrong, but stopped and thought hard about it. Was he? "We've... talked." But not like they used to. There had been nights where Jeff had passed out, or was occupied playing whatever his video game of the week was, and she and Gideon had sat and just talked. Shared things about themselves, about their dreams. She'd always chalked it up to being good friends—family, even—but even if they'd restarted their acquaintance, they hadn't reestablished the intimacy they'd once had.

Sex, yes.

Intimacy, no.

She frowned. "I guess you're right. God, I'm sorry, Gideon. I've been treating you like a prize stud."

He chuckled. "I haven't exactly complained. But

I do miss us, Lucy. Whatever version of your future you're aiming for, make room for me."

That startled a laugh out of her. "You're just as confident now as you were back then."

"Two years can change a person, but it can't *change* a person."

That was what she was afraid of. Lucy had fought hard to shed the timid woman she'd become while dating Jeff. She'd even mostly succeeded, if one didn't look too closely at her lack of dating. But she couldn't shake the fear that, deep down, she was still that mouse of a person who'd let her boyfriend say such horrible things to her—worse, who'd believed him when he did.

"I should have known." He spoke softly in the tiny space between them. "I said it before and I'll say it again—I knew Jeff was an asshole, but I didn't know the extent of it. I would have stepped in."

Her heart surged even as she shook her head. "If anyone should have seen the signs and stepped in, it was me. I let myself get taken in by him, and I almost married him because I was too stubborn and too naive to see him for what he was. If we're going to lay blame, there's plenty to go around." She covered his hand with hers. "I don't want to talk about Jeff anymore. He's taken up enough of both of our lives, and I don't want to give him even another second."

"I won't argue that." Gideon nudged her closer yet, until she was almost sitting in his lap. "I have the prettiest woman in all NYC sitting with me in a dark restaurant. I can think of a thousand things I'd rather say and do than talk about a piece of shit that we share a mutual history with."

She laid her hand on his thigh, enjoying the way the muscle clenched beneath his jeans. "I can think of a few things to add to the list." They were alone in this mini room within the restaurant. They could do anything they wanted to beneath the table and no one would be the wiser. "Gideon..." She slid her hand higher.

"Yeah?"

"What have you been up to since I saw you last?"

He blinked down at her as if he couldn't reconcile her ever-sliding hand with her words. Finally he relaxed, muscle by individual muscle. "After you and..." He looked away and back. "Two years ago, I looked at my life and decided I was done dicking around. I went after the biggest accounts I could find and went head-to-head with companies that had reputations stretching back before we were born." He laughed. "I figured I had nothing to lose, so I might as well aim for the stars."

"You've made quite the name for yourself." Even if her company didn't make a habit of contracting headhunters to fill positions, Lucy would've had to be living under a rock not to hear news of Gideon. He'd beaten out several more well-known headhunters and developed an excellent reputation in the process. He always got his man—or woman, as it were.

God help the woman he finally sets his sights on. She won't stand a chance.

The thought was bittersweet in the extreme. Lucy

cared about him. She wanted him happy…but contemplating him with another woman made her want to throw things. *Stop that.*

He's yours for the duration.

That will have to be enough.

But what if it wasn't?

CHAPTER FOURTEEN

GIDEON INSISTED ON DESSERT, if only to keep things going for a little bit longer. Lucy must have felt the same way because she didn't hesitate before she picked a particularly delicious-sounding apple cobbler to his cheesecake. The waiter—who was getting a significant tip since he'd made himself scarce in between checking on them—took their order and hurried off. The restaurant had filled up, though the only evidence of it they had was a low murmur of conversation by people they couldn't see.

He curled a strand of Lucy's hair around his finger. "You said we needed to talk."

"Don't we?"

He'd always liked Lucy's directness. Even when she was highly uncomfortable with the subject—like sex—she still made an effort to cut through the bullshit and be as honest as possible. Now he almost wished that she was willing to let the slow slide of afternoon into evening go on without following through on her words this morning. Gideon should have known better. "Yeah, we do."

She met his gaze directly, never one to shy away from a potential confrontation. "Shall I go first or shall you?"

Though he was tempted to let her take the lead, that was the coward's way out. Gideon knew what he wanted and the only way to give him a snowball's chance in hell was to go for it without reservation. So he let go of her hair and sat back. "Pick me."

She blinked and then blinked again. "I'm sorry?"

"Screw the others guys and screw the list I put together. They won't make you happy like I can, and you know it. I know you as well as anyone, and we match up in the bedroom and out of it. Pick me." *I love you. I've always loved you.* He didn't say it. He'd already pressed his luck by putting his cards on the table. If he threw that at her, she'd be gone before he finished the sentence.

She leaned forward and then shook her head. "What are you saying?"

"You know what I'm saying. I want you. You want me. We fit, Lucy. You can't deny that it's true." He held himself still in an effort to keep from reaching for her. Crowding her now was a mistake and using sex to cloud her judgment was a dick move. Not one that he was above, but if he wanted a chance—a real chance—with her, he had to do this right.

As right as he could do it when they'd started this thing with her dating another guy and then restarted it by bargaining for sex lessons in addition to her attempting to marry another man.

When you put it like that...

Lucy put her hand to her mouth and dropped it as quickly. "I don't know what to say."

Hell, he really had overplayed it. He didn't retreat farther physically, though he wanted to. Instead, Gideon gave her an easy smile. "It's fine. We're fine."

"No, I don't think we are." She rubbed her hands over her face and looked at him, her blue eyes so bleak, it broke his fucking heart. "Gideon, even with all the crap in our history and the two-year separation, you're one of the closest friends I have. I *care* about you. I don't know what I'd do if I lost our friendship again and…" Her hands fluttered between them. "We have irreconcilable differences."

"What are you talking about?" He reined in his reaction until she could tell him exactly what the hell she meant by that. *I was never on that goddamn list.*

"When's the last time you dated someone for longer than a few weeks?"

He froze. "That's the measuring stick you're going to use against me? Fine, Lucy. I haven't dated anyone for longer than a few weeks. I've been focusing on my career, and before that, it was school." He shook his head, frustration reaching a boiling point. "It's pretty rich that you expect me to roll with your limited dating history, but mine is the reason you won't consider me."

"That's not what I meant." She tucked her hair behind her ear. "Okay, it's a little what I meant, but the core concept is still the same. What happens when I throw all my other options out the window and say yes to you? Are you planning on marrying me? Because that's still the endgame, and rather quickly. Even if you *are* willing to take that step, what happens in a few weeks, months, however long, when you get bored—or, heaven forbid, you meet someone who you might actually love?" Lucy slumped in the booth. "No, it's not worth the risk. You'd realize that if you took emotion out of your reaction."

That was the problem—Gideon couldn't take emotion out of the equation when it came to Lucy. He'd never been able to. "I wouldn't do that to you."

"Maybe not intentionally. But eventually you'd resent me for pushing you into this choice."

He took a calming breath and then another. "You're not giving me much credit here, Lucy." She thought she had it all figured out, and he couldn't say a damn thing to dissuade her because it'd just be used as evidence of either how unready he was for that kind of commitment, or how much she valued their friendship. *Struck down because she cares about me.*

That brought him up short.

He was being greedy, but hell. The thought of her with someone else when they *fit* drove Gideon out of his goddamn mind. He took her hand, noting the tension there. "You've given me the worst-case scenario, and I respect that. Let me paint you a different picture."

Lucy hesitated. "Okay."

"You pick me. We get married, figure out living arrangements. Nothing bad happens. In fact, our quality of life improves exponentially. We force ourselves to take a few breaks from work a year and travel a bit. We start working through that list I know you've put together. We make our house a home. Fuck, maybe we have some kids, too. And every night, it's just us. You and me."

Her lips curved in a faint smile. "I like how you added in my sexual bucket list."

"It's important." He ran his thumb over her knuckles. Gideon wanted the life he'd just described. He wanted to be able to shoot Lucy a text and meet her after work for dinner and then walk home together and make love on every goddamn surface of the place they shared. He wanted the lazy Sunday mornings and the long weekends away. He wanted to be able to call her when he nailed an account or to get her calls when she was victorious in court.

He wanted it all.

Lucy pressed her lips together. "What if it blows apart in our face?"

"What if it doesn't?" He kept stroking her knuckles as she relaxed against him, bit by bit. "But let's talk this out your way. You pick someone else. We stop sleeping together, but that tension isn't going to disappear. Your new husband—" the term soured his stomach "—picks up on the tension and it makes him uncomfortable. Because it will, Lucy. Even if the guy is interested in marriage in name only, he'll have a problem with it."

"But—"

"Trust me. He will draw the line in the sand, and you'll have to choose which side of it you're going to be on." Gideon hated seeing the worry all over her face, but if they were being real, it had to be said. "You'll pick him. You'll have to."

The waiter walked in carrying their desserts. He set them on the table, took one look at Gideon's and Lucy's faces and stepped back. "Let me know if you need anything. Enjoy." He dashed out of the room.

"I don't... This is too much." She picked up a fork and poked at her apple cobbler. "You just dropped a serious information bomb on me and I don't even know how to wrap my head around it."

"Then don't."

She twisted to look at him. "What are you talking about?"

"I'm not saying you need to make the decision this second." He nudged his dessert away. "But you need to stop thinking that I'm not an option. I am. Fuck, I'm the best option."

"Arrogant to the very end."

"I'm sure of my worth. I'm even surer of how good we'd be. We've more than proved it over the last two weeks."

"One of which you weren't even on the same side of the country." But she relaxed against him and allowed him to tuck her head against his shoulder. "I'll think about it, Gideon. I don't... I don't know if I can promise more than that."

"Don't let fear win, Lucy. You've gone down that road before and you already know how it ends."

The walk back to Lucy's place happened in a blur. She couldn't get Gideon's words out of her head and his big presence at her side eclipsed all else. He made it sound so simple—the easiest thing in the world. *Pick me.*

It wasn't that easy.

The picture he painted was an attractive one. More than attractive. She craved that life, craved the connection already strung between her and Gideon. But Lucy had seen firsthand how bad things could get when she let someone close and they turned on her. Gideon would never cheat on her—of that, she was certain—but there were so many ways a person could hurt someone they cared about. Most of the time, it was even unintentional.

If she married some near stranger and they did something careless or cruel, she could respond without missing a beat. They weren't close enough to hurt her. Gideon, though? He could cut her to the bone.

Aren't you tired of living in fear?

The voice in her head sounded a whole lot like his. She nodded absently at the doorman and led the way into her building. Fear had controlled every choice she'd made since she'd found out Jeff had been sleeping around on her. Fear that she'd never get out had prompted her to end things in a rather remarkable fight. Fear of failure had thrust her into a career that she might love but which she'd chosen for its earning potential. Fear of being hurt again kept her from giving dating more than a token effort.

What if she just…jumped?

Lucy unlocked her door and turned to him. "Come in?"

"Sure."

His presence filled her apartment, giving it a life that it seemed to miss when it was just her and Garfunkel there. The feline in question meandered up as if he just happened to be in the room at the same time they were. She bent to pick him up and turned to face Gideon. "What if we do a trial run?"

"Trial run." Neither his tone nor his body language gave even the slightest indication of what was going on in that beautiful head of his.

"Yes, a trial run." She warmed to the idea as she spoke. "I have a few months before I'll be down to the wire on this marriage business. A week or two shouldn't make much difference."

His eyebrows rose. "What do you think you'll know in two weeks that you don't know now?"

He had a point, but she wasn't about to admit it. Making any kind of decision right that second felt like too much too soon. She'd know in a week or two. She'd be *sure*—or as sure as Lucy ever was these days about things outside of the office. "What do you say?"

"Yes." He carefully extracted Garfunkel from her arms and set the cat free. Then he set his hands on her hips and pulled her slowly toward him until they stood bare inches apart. "I say yes, Lucy. If you need two weeks to figure this out one way or another, that's what you'll have."

Her throat tightened. "You're too good to me."

"You've got that backward." He sifted his fingers through her hair, tilting her head back so she lifted her face to him. "I'm taking you to bed now."

She blinked at the change in subject. But was it really

a change at all? Anything left to say would just be rehashing what they'd already gone over. Left to her own devices, she'd drive them both crazy with her doubts. Better to let their obvious physical connection take over and push her worries to the back seat than to sabotage things before they had a chance to get started.

Gideon didn't wait for a response before sweeping her into his arms and striding back to her room. He carefully kicked the door shut, his gaze on the floor. "Woke up this morning to the damn cat watching me."

"He does that." She dragged her fingers through his hair and kissed his neck. "In his defense, you look absolutely marvelous while you sleep."

"You watched me while I slept?" He set her on the bed and backed up enough to pull her boots off, quickly followed by her leggings. "That's very creepy of you."

"You're in my apartment—that means I'm not creepy." She pulled her shirt off and tossed it away. "If I was standing on the fire escape outside your window and doing it, *that* would be creepy."

"A fair point." He nudged her onto her back and stripped slowly.

Lucy propped herself on her elbows. "Have I mentioned lately how much I enjoy you in flannel?"

"It might have come up once or twice." He dropped the shirt onto the floor and started on his jeans. "Careful there, or you might look up one day and realize I've grown a beard and started wearing thick-rimmed black glasses."

She laughed. "You don't even need glasses."

"My point stands." He hooked the back of her thighs and slid her farther onto the bed. She expected him to follow her to the mattress, but Gideon stepped back. He pointed at her. "Don't move."

"Okay..." She froze when he went to her nightstand and unerringly opened the bottom drawer. When he straightened, he had her pink vibrator in his hand. She shivered. "Oh."

He examined it. "This isn't a design I'm familiar with."

"You—"

He chuckled. "Give me some credit. I can figure out how it works." He thumbed it on, his grin widening. "Brilliant." He joined her on the bed and took up a position next to her with his head propped on his hand. "Spread your legs."

"This feels..." When he didn't immediately jump in, she had to search for something to fill the space. "Naughty." It wasn't quite the right word, but it fit.

"More or less than bending over that table and offering your ass to me?"

Her entire body went hot at both the memory and his words. "I'm not sure. It's not the same thing." There was no one here except them. No one to potentially walk in or witness. It didn't make the encounter less hot, but it had a different flavor as a result.

Gideon traced her puckered nipples with his gaze. "More or less than stroking yourself on a video chat with me?"

She gave a mock frown even as her breathing picked up. "You've made your point."

"Have I?" He ran his thumb over the circular silicone portion of the vibrator. "I still have a few points to make. Spread your legs wider."

She paused just long enough to have his brows slant down—the reaction she was aiming for—and then obeyed. The heat in his dark eyes was nothing compared to the inferno blasting into existence beneath her skin. *What if it was always like this?* He pressed the vibrator to her clit before the thought could take root. The silicone perfectly circled her clit, the vibrations drawing a moan from her lips. The fact that it was *Gideon* wielding it only made the entire situation that much hotter.

"How often do you use this on yourself?"

She arched half off the bed when he lifted it away. "Often. Don't tease me. I was so close."

He grinned wickedly. "I know."

"Gideon." She couldn't stand the teasing even as she loved it.

"Next time we go out—" he touched the vibrator to her clit long enough to have pleasure almost cresting and then took it away again "—wear what I bought you today under your dress. Halfway through dinner, I'm going to tell you to take off your panties and slip them into my pocket."

She couldn't catch her breath. "Tricky."

"I have a better idea." He set the toy aside and idly stroked her with his fingers. "There's a blackout restaurant I've been interested in trying."

How he could talk so calmly when she was in

danger of going out of her skin was beyond her. "Gideon—"

He shoved two fingers into her, drawing a cry from her lips. "I'll spend the entire dinner fucking you with my fingers right there at the table. You'll have to be quiet or the other diners will hear you." He stroked her and slid her wetness up to circle her clit before pushing back into her again. "Though, if *they're* too quiet, they'll be able to hear exactly what I'm doing to you."

She reached for him, only to have him use his free hand to press the vibrator into hers. "Show me."

It took three tries to get her shaking fingers to operate it while he kept fucking her with his fingers the same way he'd described. She could picture exactly how it would feel to sit in perfect darkness, her dress up around the tops of her thighs, Gideon's big hand palming her pussy as he gave the waiter their order with none the wiser. She froze. "Don't the waitstaff have night-vision goggles?"

He guided her hand with the vibrator to her clit, waiting until she'd placed it perfectly to respond. "Yes. They'll be able to see every single thing I'm doing to you."

Her orgasm exploded through her. Lucy's back bowed and she fumbled the toy, but Gideon was there, his fingers still inside her as he repositioned it and sent another wave of pure bliss through her. "Oh, my God." She thrashed, though she couldn't say if she was trying to get away from him or closer. "Oh, God. Gideon. Please. Stop. Don't stop."

A thunk sounded as the vibrator hit the floor and

then his mouth was there, soothing her oversensitized clit in long strokes. She laced her fingers through his hair, riding his face. "What are you doing to me? I don't… I feel completely out of control."

He lifted his head just enough to say, "I have no control with you, either, Lucy. I feel like a fucking animal. I can't get enough of you."

"Then get up here." She tugged on his hair. "You want me? Then take me."

Gideon hadn't bothered with a plan when it came to seducing Lucy into seeing things his way. All his damn plans went right out the window the second their clothes came off. Now, looking up her body into those blue eyes demanding he take her, he wished for a plan. This whole day was special. The start of their trial run. But more than that, it was the first time they'd spent time together without someone else between them.

Just Gideon and Lucy.

He wanted her to know how important that was to him, how close to perfect today had been. How much he cared about her. How much he wanted her in every way, body and soul.

In the end, Gideon did the only thing he could do. He crawled up her body and kissed her. She met him eagerly, her body already shifting to accommodate his, her legs wrapping around his waist and her hands coasting down his back to dig her fingers into his ass. As if they'd done this a thousand times before and would do it another thousand times.

"Condom," he rasped.

"I'm clean." Her lips brushed his with every word. "And…well, I'm on birth control."

He went still. "What are you saying?" There was no room for misunderstanding—not here, not now.

Lucy kissed one side of his mouth and then the other. "If…"

"I'm clean. I haven't been with anyone since the last time I was tested." He hadn't done anything to disabuse her of the notion since it'd be wasted breath, but Gideon hadn't had much interest in sleeping around in the last couple of years. He hadn't been celibate, but the demon driving him had disappeared right around the time Lucy had vanished from his life.

"I don't want barriers between us. I want you—all of you."

He wanted that, too. So bad, he could fucking taste it. "You're sure."

She wedged her hand between them and stroked his cock once, twice, before guiding him to her entrance. "I'm sure."

He didn't ask again. Gideon kissed her as he slid into her, inch by inch. There were no words to express his feelings at her trust in him. From the very beginning, she'd trusted him, but this was something else entirely. He kissed her with everything he had, everything he couldn't say. And then he began to move.

She rose to meet each thrust, their bodies moving in a dance as old as time, neither of them willing to break the kiss. He laced his fingers through her hair to tip her face for a better angle. She raked her nails over his ass, urging him to move faster, harder.

It was like flipping a switch.

He froze for one eternal second. Lucy nipped his bottom lip. "Stop being so careful with me. I can take it."

He knew that. Of course he knew that. Gideon tightened his grip on her hair with one hand, tilting her head to the side so he had access to her neck. He dragged his mouth down the line and then bit her shoulder. "Teeth?"

"Yes." She let loose a shaky laugh. "Just don't mark up where anyone can see."

Which was as good as saying that she *did* want him to mark her somewhere.

Gideon rolled onto his back, taking her with him, and slammed her down onto his cock. "Fuck me." He sat up enough to palm her breasts as she did what he commanded. Gideon sucked her nipple hard, urged on by her fingers in his hair and her hips slamming down onto him again and again. He took as much of her breast into his mouth as he could and bit her. Lucy cried out, her pussy squeezing him as she came.

He wasn't through.

He flopped her onto her stomach and yanked her to the edge of the bed. Gideon guided his cock back into her, paused to kick her feet a little wider and press his hand to the small of her back, and then he started to move.

He fucked her. There was no other word for it. She wanted it hard, and her hands fisting her comforter and the cries slipping from her lips only drove him on. He became a wild thing, slamming into her over and over again, driven toward a release he couldn't have stopped if he'd tried.

It wasn't enough. He was so damn close, and it wasn't enough.

Gideon covered her with his body, reaching around to bracket her throat with one hand while he slipped the other between her thighs and pinched her clit. "You're mine, Lucy. *Mine.*" The move bent her backward and she twisted to give him her mouth.

"Yes, yes." She bucked against him, grinding herself against his hand. "Yours. Always. God, Gideon, don't stop."

"Never. I'll never fucking stop."

CHAPTER FIFTEEN

A LAZY SUNDAY morning was the only thing Gideon wanted, but he'd agreed to breakfast with Roman weeks ago. He left Lucy a note and brewed her a pot of coffee before heading out. An hour—two, tops—and he'd be back with her. Simple.

He still had to talk himself out of turning around seven different times during the cab ride—and again when he climbed out onto the sidewalk. The limited timeline Lucy gave him rattled around in his head, and he had the irrational fear that if he didn't spend every second with her that he could scrape out, it wouldn't be enough and she'd leave.

She's not leaving yet. I have time.

Not enough. Never enough.

Roman stood outside the little hole-in-the-wall place, staring at a pair of guys smoking just down the way. Gideon stopped next to him. "You quit."

"I know that. Doesn't mean I don't miss it sometimes."

"Miss the ability to breathe a whole lot more when you end up with lung cancer."

Roman rolled his hazel eyes. "Yeah, got it. Thanks, Mom."

"How's your mother doing?"

"Same as always. *Just swimmingly, darling.*" He gave a spot-on impression of his mother's breathy, high voice. Roman opened the door. "She and my old man are on that goddamn yacht somewhere. The Caribbean this week—either Saint Lucia or Jamaica."

"Worse ways to spend your retirement." He followed his friend into the brightly lit restaurant. If one could call Frank's a restaurant. There were exactly two tables and three chairs, and in all Gideon's time of coming here, he'd never seen them empty. Most people took their food to go, which was what he and Roman did. They turned left without bothering to talk about it—it was always the direction they took when they managed to carve time out of their schedules for this sort of thing.

They both finished their breakfast sandwiches by the end of the first block. Roman barely waited for them to cross the street before he started in. "What are you doing with Lucy?"

"None of your damn business."

"No, it's not, but you know me well enough to know that I'm not going to leave it alone. Explain. Now."

Gideon stopped walking and turned to face his friend. He didn't like the set of Roman's jaw or the tight way he held himself. "Why are you pissed?"

"Everyone with eyes in their head has seen the way you've watched her since she came into our group.

You've had a thing for her for as long as we've known her."

He crossed his arms over his chest. "You have a point. Get to it."

"My point is that you agreed to find her a husband—that's it. A husband that is from the agreed-upon list that I helped you put together." When he didn't immediately jump in, Roman glared. "I may be pretty, but I'm not stupid. You dragged her into the back room at Vortex and you two had sex, which means you've crossed so many damn lines, you're too deep into it to realize exactly how much you're fucking up."

He wasn't fucking up. He might have changed the rules with her, but she was on the same page he was. *More or less.* It was the "less" that worried Gideon. Lucy had put it all out there yesterday—her fears about the future and what it might mean for them—and he'd essentially steamrolled her.

Admitting that to himself and admitting it to Roman were two very different things.

Roman, damn him, knew it. He shook his head. "She gave you an opening and you just went for it, didn't you? Didn't bother to stop and think about the damage you were dealing because you were too busy thinking with your cock."

Enough was enough. "I would never hurt Lucy."

"You're hurting her *right now.*" Roman raked his hand through his hair. "We all stood by while that piece of shit ran around on her, and we have to live with that. There's no making it right—not really—but she came to you for help, Gideon. You do anything else than give her exactly the help she wanted and you're just as bad as he is."

No need to clarify the "he" Roman meant. Gideon gave his head a sharp shake. "It's not the same."

"Isn't it? You and me—and even him, though I hate to include Jeff in anything—are not good men. We're just not. We never have been—you don't get as far in the world as we've gotten without throwing people under the bus along the way. I've made my peace with that, and I thought you had, too, but you've always had a white knight complex when it came to Lucy. *She* is good—as good as anyone is. She deserves a hell of a lot better than she's gotten up to this point, and that means we owe her."

"Fuck, will you listen to yourself?" Gideon knew all that. How could he not, when he'd thought it himself over and over again for years? But hearing Roman say it felt different. Real. As if Gideon really had been deluding himself all this time by thinking things could work out between him and Lucy. "She and I just work."

Roman's eyes didn't hold a shred of sympathy. "For how long? How long until she wakes up one morning and realizes you pulled one over on her? She asked you for help, and instead of doing what you promised, you used her needing you to leverage a place in her life. That's shitty, Gideon. If our positions were reversed, you'd tell me the same thing."

He started to react, but stopped short. If Roman had come to him with news that Lucy had approached him for help, and he'd ended up sleeping with her and sabotaging her matchmaking plans… "I would have punched you in those perfect teeth."

Roman rubbed his jaw. "You have a wicked right hook."

He didn't smile, though it couldn't be more obvious that his friend was trying to lighten the mood.

Gideon tossed his garbage into a trash can and stared at the street. "I didn't set out to do this." *I love her.* But what did his feelings matter when he hadn't taken hers into account? Lucy'd had years of playing second fiddle to some asshole—she didn't need Gideon coming in and starting a replay, regardless of his intentions. He'd never cheat on her, would do everything in his power to make her happy.

She didn't choose me.

That was what it came down to. If she'd given him any indication that she had started this process with some sort of feelings for him beyond friendship, he would have a right to ask for more. Yesterday she'd even gone so far as to try to explain that she didn't want to lose him as a friend, and he'd leveraged that fear into getting her to agree to give them a trial run.

His shoulders slumped. "Fuck me, you're right."

"I'm not saying it to be a dick." For once, Roman sounded downright apologetic. "You're my friend, and if she was any other woman, I'd say to hell with her plans—play dirty. But this isn't any other woman. This is Lucy we're talking about."

And, because it was Lucy, that changed everything.

Gideon took out his phone and stared at it for a few

moments. He knew what he had to do. The honorable thing—the thing he'd promised to do.

He had to set her up with another man.

Lucy woke up disorientated. The day before had been an emotional roller coaster, and she'd seriously looked forward to spending a lazy Sunday with Gideon, letting their time together ease her concerns over the whole thing.

Then she'd woken up alone.

She touched the side of the bed Gideon had slept on, but it was long since cold. Telling herself there was nothing to worry about, she went through her morning routine and then headed into the kitchen. A full pot of coffee sat waiting, along with a sticky note with a hastily written explanation. "Breakfast with Roman. Back soon." Lucy smiled a little and poured herself a cup of coffee. If he was occupied for a little bit, it wouldn't hurt to check her emails and make sure there was nothing requiring her immediate attention.

He still hadn't arrived by the time she was done with that, so she scrambled up a pair of eggs and went back to work on her files. Normally she had no problem losing herself in the facts she was compiling, but Lucy couldn't help keeping one eye on the clock as an hour stretched into two.

Did Gideon feel as strangely about what happened yesterday as she did?

Maybe he had regrets.

She wished he was there so his presence could keep her from second-guessing every single thing she'd said or done yesterday. Had she been too honest at dinner? He'd said he wanted honesty, but there was honesty and *honesty.* The sex had been even more outstanding than she'd come to expect, both the tender touches and murmured words and the rough and possessive...

"Stop it." She poured herself a third cup of coffee and headed for her living room. Obsessing over what Gideon did or did not regret would only drive her crazy. *Crazier.*

Work would steady her. Work *always* steadied her. It was her job that had gotten her through the worst times of her life, the ability to lose herself in the facts and how to use them to create the story she wanted the judge or jury to believe.

Except this time it didn't work.

Lucy kept glancing at her phone, waiting for a call or a text or, hell, a smoke signal. Something from Gideon. Something to prove that he didn't think this whole thing was a terrible mistake. Something to reassure *her* from deciding she needed to find a different way to accomplish her aims.

When her phone finally buzzed, she dropped the paper she'd been staring at for five minutes without reading and snatched it up. It was from Gideon, but only a few words.

The Blue Lagoon 7pm.

She hesitated, wondering if she'd missed something, and typed out a quick reply.

Dinner?

Yes. Wear something nice.

Lucy waited, but no information was forthcoming. She glanced at the clock. Two hours until he wanted her there. *Where has the day gone?* She could keep pretending to work, but the nerves bouncing in her stomach spoke of the futility of it. Something had changed with Gideon, and she wasn't sure it was a good sign.

Yesterday he'd been almost in her face with how much he wanted her—wanted *this*—and now he was playing least-in-sight. She'd thought Gideon was too direct a man to ever disappear on a woman, but she should have known better.

She'd watched him do it before, hadn't she?

She and Jeff even used to joke about the Gideon Special. He'd grow distant from whoever he was dating, showing up more and more at their place, and if the woman didn't allow him to fade gracefully away, he'd take her out for dinner and cut it off.

Kind of like the dinner he had planned with Lucy tonight.

She shot to her feet. "No. I'm being paranoid." Gideon wouldn't have said the things he'd said if he was planning on turning around and dumping her on her ass. He wouldn't have changed the perfectly good set of rules to push her to put her heart on the line.

Oh, my God. My heart is on the line.

She sat down heavily. She'd known she cared about

him, of course—hard to be friends and not care about someone—but her heart being in danger had nothing to do with friendship and everything to do with deeper feelings.

Real feelings.

The same kinds of feelings that made a person blind to another's faults and left them emotionally bloodied and bruised. She didn't want that. She'd actively worked to *avoid* that.

And yet here she was.

She got ready, mostly to escape the doubt plaguing her. It was fear talking—it had to be. Having a meltdown about their first speed bump during this trial dating thing they had going was just going to prove how unready to date or marry Lucy really was.

Obviously something had come up with Gideon that required his attention and prevented him from coming back to spend the day with her. Just as obviously, if it was important enough to need his presence then it would make his sending her a bunch of texts impossible. He'd arranged dinner tonight and paused in whatever he was doing long enough to let her know that they had plans, and *that* was a good sign.

She was overreacting.

Simple.

But she didn't feel any better two hours later when she stood in front of the Blue Lagoon, shivering in the cold beneath her thick coat. *This is fine. Everything is fine.* She walked inside and gave Gideon's name. The host smiled welcomingly and led her to a semi-private corner.

Lucy caught sight of a man sitting there already, but her steps stuttered when she realized he wasn't Gideon. *What the hell?* There was nothing to do but keep following the host. She started to reach for his arm to let him know that there had been some mistake, but as they came even with the table, she recognized the man. *Aaron Livingston.*

No. Oh, Gideon. Why?

She had to fight to keep her expression neutral as Aaron rose and smiled. "Lucy, it's been a while."

"I'm surprised you remember." She let him pull out her chair, her mind racing a million miles a minute. Gideon had set this up. It should have gone without saying, but she still couldn't wrap her mind around it. Twelve hours ago he'd told her that he wanted her to pick him—only him—and now he'd set her up with another man.

Aaron resumed his seat. "It's been a few years, but you're not a woman one forgets." He smiled charmingly, and though she could recognize why *BuzzFeed* had labeled him one of the hottest bachelors in NYC, his perfect features did nothing for her.

They also did nothing to explain why he was *here*.

You know why he's here, just like you know what it means.

If she was a better person, she'd sit and make small talk with Aaron and keep her eye on the prize—the whole reason she'd put this plan into motion in the first place. A husband.

But Lucy couldn't focus on anything beyond the fact that Gideon had set her up. She lasted a full thirty seconds before she pushed back her chair and rose. "I am so sorry, Aaron, but I've got to go."

"Go…?" Those keen dark eyes took her in. "You didn't realize you were meeting me, did you?"

"I'm really very sorry." She headed for the exit as quickly as she could without actually running. Lucy made it onto the street before she found her phone at the bottom of her purse. She dialed Gideon's number and listened to it ring and ring and ring before clicking over to voice mail. She hung up without leaving a message.

That was the moment she should have stopped. It was clear Gideon didn't want her, that he'd misled her horribly. She didn't give a flying fuck. He didn't get to put her in this position and then avoid dealing with the fallout.

She scrolled through her contacts to find Roman's number. It wasn't one she'd used more than once, and that was years ago when she'd planned Jeff's surprise birthday party. *I was such an idiot. Apparently, I am* still *an idiot.* She dialed, holding her breath as it rang. He'd probably changed his number by now—most people did at one time or another.

But she recognized the cultured, masculine voice that answered. "Lucy?"

She lifted her arm to hail a cab. "You're going to tell me where he is, Roman, and you're going to tell me right this instant."

CHAPTER SIXTEEN

THE SECOND GIDEON heard the buzzer being pressed repeatedly, he knew it was Lucy. He hadn't even tried to hide. He'd known what he was doing today and, as sick to his stomach as it made him, Roman was right—it was the right thing to do. Hurt her a little now and set her back on the path she'd carved out for herself.

Knowing that did nothing to prepare him for the fury on her face when he opened the door. "Lucy."

"No, you do not get to *Lucy* me as if nothing's changed." She pushed into the apartment and spun to face him. "What the hell was that tonight, Gideon?"

He kept his expression stoic, knowing it would make everything worse. "I'm just doing what you contracted me for."

She actually took a step back. "You've got to be kidding me. You're going to take that stance now? What happened to you wanting me to pick *you*?"

"I was wrong." It actually hurt to say the words aloud, and it hurt more to see the naked pain on her face. He forced himself to keep talking. *A little hurt now, rather than a big hurt later.* "This was fun, but you were right when you pointed out that I'm not the keeping kind." She'd survived her breakup with Jeff. She'd bounce back even faster from this mistake with him.

Because that was how she'd see it in a few weeks—a mistake, a bullet dodged.

"You're serious." Lucy shook her head. "What happened between leaving my bed and writing me a note and..." She trailed off. "What did Roman say to you?"

She always had been smart. He let nothing show on his face. "He didn't have to say anything. A little distance was all I needed to realize that we aren't suited."

"Aren't suited." She pressed a hand to her chest as if he'd reached out and hit her there. Gideon felt like he had. She finally took a deep breath and lifted her chin. "You're a coward, Gideon Novak."

He flinched. "What the hell are you talking about?"

"You. Are. A. Coward." He could actually see her putting the pieces of herself back into place, though her bottom lip quivered, just a little. "Last night was too good and, I'll be honest—it scared me, too. But the difference between you and me is that *I* fought that fear and focused on how good it could be." She raked him with her gaze. "I'm not fighting for this. I spent too long fighting to be with someone who didn't even try. I won't do that again, Gideon. This was barely a bump in the road and you've already jumped ship. Fine. So be it." Her lower lip quivered again, but she made an obvious effort to still it. "I chose you, and you didn't choose me."

It felt like she'd stabbed him and twisted the blade. "Lucy—"

"No. Your actions speak just as clearly as your words and I'm not stupid. I understand." She drew herself up. "Consider our contract terminated. Keep the fee for all I care, as long as I never see you again."

Gideon watched her walk out of his apartment—and out of his life. He shut the door softly behind her and walked to his kitchen and stared blankly out the window. *It's done.* Something that took so much effort to coax into being, decimated in the course of a single day.

He braced his hands on the edge of the counter, an anchor to keep from chasing her down and trying to explain. There was no explaining this in a way that accomplished the severing of their relationship and left her pissed off enough to leave him behind for good. As much as he'd hated hearing it, Roman was right. Gideon hadn't been thinking straight from the second Lucy contacted him. If he had been, he would have set her up with someone else for her matchmaking needs. He wasn't qualified for either of the things she needed from him, and he sure as fuck wasn't an unbiased party.

Letting his own selfish needs overshadow hers, and then convincing her to see things his way…

Yeah, there was no explaining that away. Cutting Lucy loose was the best thing he could have done for her.

He let his head drop between his shoulders. The best thing for Lucy, but he'd be riding this wave of pain for the foreseeable future. Getting out of town might help, but the memories of what they'd done here and elsewhere would still be waiting to ambush him when he returned.

No, better to stay and push through the worst of it.

A band around his chest formed, blisteringly hot and so tight he exhaled in a rush. He'd just ended things with Lucy.

Ended for good.

Gideon slumped against the counter. He'd known that woman for six damn years. Had been respectful of her relationship with Jeff and never said so much as a word out of line. Had backed the fuck off and left her alone after things had imploded so she wouldn't have to look at his face and see a constant reminder of the lies she'd fielded.

Through it all, a small part of him had been sure that it would work out. One way or another, he'd find a path to Lucy. That he'd win her if he was just patient enough.

He huffed out a pained laugh. He should have known better. He'd been so busy putting her on a pedestal, he hadn't stopped to ask what *she* wanted. Worse. He'd ignored what she'd wanted in favor of his own desires being met.

She hadn't picked him.

If he hadn't forced the issue, if he'd just stayed in the place she'd designated for him, he could have maintained their friendship. Would it be painful watching her marry another man? Fuck yes. It would have ripped his still-beating heart out of his chest to smile and congratulate her on picking a man who'd do as a husband.

But less painful than standing there, realizing he was never going to see her again.

Lucy wandered the streets for hours. She'd intended to go home, but the thought of four walls closing her in was too much to bear. It wasn't any better on the street—the city itself boxed her into place, preventing her from running until she couldn't breathe, couldn't think, was too tired to process the level of Gideon's betrayal.

He blamed himself for not telling her about Jeff's cheating sooner. She knew that. She'd even used that to ensure he wouldn't say no to helping her.

She'd also foolishly assumed that, when push came to shove, he'd get over it.

Lucy looked up and breathed a sigh that wasn't quite relief. She dug out her phone and called. Her sister answered on the first ring. "What's up?"

"I don't suppose you're home?"

All joking disappeared from Becka's voice. "Yes. What's wrong? What happened?"

Burning started in her throat, making it hard to swallow. "Buzz me up?"

"Yeah, right away."

She hung up before her sister's concern had her breaking down in the street. The walk up the rickety stairs to the tiny apartment Becka insisted she loved was a lesson in torture. As if her body knew she was almost safe and had decided now was the perfect time to break down completely.

Becka opened the door as she lifted her hand to knock. Her sister wore a pair of brightly printed workout pants and a sports bra with more straps than was strictly necessary. Lucy stopped short. “You have class.”

“I already got someone to cover for me, so don’t even think of turning around.” She stepped back. “Now, get in here and tell me everything while I make some tea I threw together this weekend.”

That almost brought a smile to Lucy’s face. “Is it better than the last batch?”

“The last batch was the exception to the rule, though thank you very much for reminding me of it.” She made a face. “I couldn’t get the taste of licorice out of my mouth for days, no matter how many times I brushed my teeth and drowned myself in mouthwash.”

“Live and learn.” Her voice caught, because living and learning was exactly what Lucy *hadn’t* done. She’d been so sure she knew her path, and yet the first chance she had to take a detour that would ruin everything, she’d jumped in headfirst.

“Sit. Immediately.” Becka took her coat and purse and tossed them onto the threadbare couch. Then she guided Lucy into a chair at the small dining room table and headed for the stove. The loft apartment meant Lucy only had to rotate a little to keep her sister in view.

Becka got hot water going in an ancient-looking kettle and doled out loose leaf tea into two wire tea steepers. The few minutes it took to get the water boiling was enough to calm Lucy's racing thoughts a little. "I'm sorry to drop in like this."

"What are sisters for if not to be there when you need them?" Becka poured the hot water into two mugs and brought them to the table. "This is about Gideon."

She started to deny it, but what was the point? She'd locked down everything after the Jeff fiasco, and all it had done was completely isolate her from the world. Maybe talking through it with her sister was the right choice.

"I… He changed the rules on me. I had a fully fleshed-out plan, and every intention of following through on it, but I didn't anticipate *him*. Our connection. He showed every evidence of wanting more with me—we even talked about it and he said so in as many words—and then I wake up this morning to find him gone." She had to stop and focus on breathing for several moments. Even with the break, when she spoke again, her voice was strained. "I thought we were meeting tonight, but when I showed up to dinner, he'd set me up with another man."

Becka's blue eyes, so like Lucy's, went wide. "I think you're going to have to rewind to the part when you woke up alone. You had *sex* with Gideon?"

She'd left out that part of the plan, hadn't she? Lucy cleared her throat and stared at the ever-darkening water of her tea. "We've been sleeping together since the initial agreement. It started out as a way to get my confidence back sexually, but things…changed."

"They'll do that when sex is involved." She shot her sister a look, and Becka gave her wide eyes. "Not that I would know, of course. Your dear little sister is most definitely one hundred percent a virgin."

She snorted. "I'd believe that if I hadn't caught you and...what was his name?"

"Johnny Cash." Becka laughed. "Don't look at me like that. I know it wasn't his real name, but I was eighteen and he was hot." Her smile fell away. "So Gideon pulled a bait and switch on you? That's seriously shitty, Lucy. I never pegged him for the type to play games like that, but I've been wrong before."

"We Baudin women don't have the best of tastes in men."

"You can say that again."

She was tempted to let them skirt into safer territory, but the raw feeling inside her only got worse with each minute that passed.

Lucy pulled her mug closer. "I promised myself that I wouldn't fall in love again—that I wouldn't even put myself in the position to do so. Feelings and caring on that depth only cause pain. I didn't expect him. I couldn't fight against the connection or the way he made me feel." The burning in her throat got worse. "I thought we had a chance, Becka. A real chance. That maybe I didn't miss my chance at a happily-ever-after, and maybe it could be with Gideon."

"Oh, Lucy."

She laughed, the sound vaguely liquid with unshed tears. "That's very foolish, isn't it?"

"It's hopeful. There's nothing wrong with hope."

Except it was hope that had gotten her into this situation. It was because of hope that every beat of her heart felt as if someone were stabbing her. Hope had driven her to lay her heart bare for Gideon, and it'd gotten crushed in the process.

She took a drink, ignoring the way the hot water scalded her mouth. A small pain compared to her emotional wounds. "Screw hope. I want nothing to do with it anymore."

CHAPTER SEVENTEEN

GIDEON DIDN'T LOOK up as the door to his office slammed open. "Whatever it is, I don't want to hear about it." Keeping the damn door shut in the first place should have been enough to discourage anyone from coming in—anyone except Roman, that was.

But when he finally looked up, it wasn't Roman kicking the door shut behind him.

It was Becka Baudin.

He stared for a long moment and shook his head. "No. Whatever you have to say to me has already been said, so get out."

"It might have been said, but it wasn't said by me." She ignored his command and marched over to drop into the chair across the desk. She wore tennis shoes and neon-green workout shorts tiny enough to have him concerned about frostbite. When she shrugged out of her huge coat, she revealed a fitted tank top in an equally eye-searing pink. How it managed not to clash with her bright blue hair was beyond him.

"What the hell are you doing, walking around New

York in *January* wearing that? You're going to freeze your ass off."

She blinked and then shook her head. "You have a lot of nerve. I could appreciate that if you weren't such an overbearing, selfish asshole." Becka jumped back to her feet. Gideon caught several of the men from the cubicles gravitating toward the windows of his office and stalked over to close the blinds.

"Put on some damn clothes."

She pointed at him. "Sit your ass down and listen to what I have to say, and then I'll leave and take my apparently inadequately clothed body with me." Becka pulled her ponytail tighter. "What the hell are you doing with my sister?"

"Nothing."

"No, shit." She looked like she wanted to throw something at him. "You know, Lucy doesn't get why you pulled that sneaky little trick with the date."

"I—"

"But *I* do." Becka paced from one side of his office to the other. "I might not have been around her and Jeff as much as you were, but I was around enough. I know you've been holding a flame for my big sister for years, and I know *you* were the one who broke the news to her about Jeff being a cheating bastard."

He started to cut in, but she spoke over him. Again. "That must have been a head trip for you, huh? Hard to break up their relationship, even if it was the right thing to do, because you were in love with your cheating best friend's girl. That muddies the waters."

"Actually—"

"I am not through." She glared, her blue eyes practically luminescent. "When I'm done talking, then you get to talk. Until then, sit down and shut up."

He didn't sit, but he did give her a short nod. Obviously she wasn't going to be deterred from whatever she was trying to accomplish. After what he'd done to Lucy, the least he could do was stand here and take a verbal lashing from her sister. "Fine."

"Good." She took another lap from one side of his office to the other. "So, you're carrying around a boatload of guilt, and playing the martyr and letting her try to move on with her life." She shot him a look. "Martyrs aren't sexy, by the way."

She sure as hell wasn't holding back. "Noted."

"So, as my sister is telling me the insane deal she put together with you, I can't help wondering what your motivation was. For screwing her, I get that—it was fulfilling a lifelong dream."

He couldn't let that stand. "No."

She stopped. "No? Which part? Screwing my sister being a lifelong dream or—"

"Stop saying that. Fuck, Becka. I didn't manipulate your sister into bed with me. *She* came to *me*."

She propped her hands on her hips. "Aha. It wasn't the sex, then. It's the guilt." She pursed her lips. "Guilt isn't any sexier than martyrdom."

"Why are you here, Becka?" He needed her to get to the point of this verbal thrashing so she'd leave. She wasn't saying anything Gideon hadn't already gone over more times than he could count. He'd replayed every step and second-guessed every action. It all added up to a mistake he couldn't take back.

He still wasn't sure if the mistake was agreeing to help Lucy—or leaving her.

"My point is that you love the shit out of my sister and have for years, but you decided to be the guilty martyr and make an executive decision about what she *should* have." She stared him down. "Tell me I'm wrong."

"She should—"

"Sweet baby Jesus." Becka rolled her eyes. "Here's a tip—take 'should' out of your vocabulary when you talk about my sister and her future. You might care about her, but ultimately, you don't get a vote. She's an adult. She can make her own choices. And she chose *you*, you asshat." She shook her head. "The question is whether *you* are willing to choose her instead of your idealized version of her." She snatched up her coat. "If I had a mic, I'd drop it, but you get the picture. Woman up or don't, but unless you have a good grovel prepared, I don't want to ever hear about you contacting my sister again." She strode out the door, leaving a trail of startled and appreciative gazes behind her.

Gideon dropped into the chair behind his desk and stared at his dark monitor. Becka hadn't said anything he didn't already know. And yet…

And yet.

He drummed his fingers on the desk. The last twenty-four hours since the fallout with Lucy had been the worst of his life. He hadn't slept. Food wasn't of interest. He hadn't even been able to work up the resolve to get good and drunk. Every time he turned around, he caught a trail of her summery scent, and the few times he'd been on the street, he'd looked for her distinctive stride even though he knew better.

He'd had his dream in the flesh—Lucy in his bed and in his life—and it'd been better than he could have imagined. He already knew she was driven and kind and had a sense of humor. He knew she loved Chinese takeout and discovering little hole-in-the-wall restaurants no one had ever heard of. He knew her parents were MIA, but she had a wonderful relationship with her sister.

He couldn't have anticipated the passion that flared between them. Hoped, yes, but even that hadn't encompassed reality. Lucy met him every step of the way, *challenged* him every step of the way. She brought fun into the bedroom even as she made him crazy in the best way possible.

And now he'd never touch her again. He'd never be able to show her a new place that he discovered. Never call just to chat with her because he was thinking of her. Never spend those fantasy lazy Sundays they kept talking about.

He'd done that.

There's no one to blame here but me. I had it all and I shit it away.

Even if he tried to make things right, Lucy would likely tell him to get lost. She *should* tell him...

He went still. *Fuck me, Becka is right.* He and Lucy had been doing just fine before he'd started obsessing over what *should* happen rather than what *was* happening.

He'd done this. He'd ruined it.

Gideon had known that, but the truth drove home hard enough to have him rubbing the back of his hand across his mouth. He felt like the biggest piece of shit in existence to have been so close to everything he'd ever dreamed of romantically and for *him* to have been the one that made it combust.

He drummed his fingers faster.

Could he fix this?

Should—

No. There was no more room for *should*. He was head over heels in love with Lucy. If she'd have him—if she'd forgive him once again—he'd do everything in his power to ensure that he never hurt her again. Not like this. Never like this.

He straightened. He'd fix it. Tonight.

Right now.

CHAPTER EIGHTEEN

LUCY CRASHED AND burned in court. There was no other way to describe it. She'd bungled the opening statement and then made an ass of herself getting into it with the prosecuting attorney until the judge called a recess until the following day. She strode out of the courtroom, her throat tight with shame and her skin hot. *I screwed up.*

No matter how frustrating or crazy her personal life got, she had always—*always*—found refuge in work. With her clients, the world made sense. It didn't matter what case they had leveled against them, she had a knack for finding the right facts to turn things in their favor. That click was her favorite thing in the world.

She'd lost it.

Two days since Gideon had unceremoniously dumped her, and she'd spent the entire time going through too many boxes of Kleenex and watching movie after movie while clutching Garfunkel. She hadn't touched her files. She hadn't checked her email. She hadn't done anything other than sit there and feel sorry for herself.

It didn't make *sense*. Work was her everything.

Work was the reason she had contacted Gideon to begin with. Dropping the ball there was inexcusable.

Why? Why can't I focus?

She knew the answer. She didn't want to face it.

But Lucy couldn't keep on like this indefinitely. If she didn't recover tonight and fix the mess she'd made today, she could kiss her promotion goodbye and it would all be for nothing. Facing down the ugly truth required more courage than she thought she had.

She hit the street and turned a direction at random, needing the movement to untangle her thoughts. Three blocks later and she was no closer to unveiling the truth.

Coward. Just like you called him.

Damn it. Lucy stopped short. "I love him." The comment earned her a few looks from people walking around her, but she started moving again before anyone could get pissed about her being a human roadblock. *I love him.*

She'd loved Jeff, but it was…different. Even if they'd been planning their wedding when she'd found out that he'd cheated on her, her connection with Jeff had never come close to what she felt for Gideon. Her heartbreak at the time hadn't made her miss a step at work. If anything, without the stress of trying to juggle her emotions over Jeff's nasty comments, she'd been free to focus solely on what was most important—her job.

The only problem? Her job didn't hold up against what she felt for Gideon. Every time she tried to work, she caught herself wondering where he was or what he was doing—or who he might be with.

The last was her own personal demon. Lucy didn't think for a minute that Gideon had dropped her on her ass and gone off to hook up with someone else. No matter what he'd said about not being the keeping kind, it was his fear talking—not reality.

He cared about her. He wouldn't have taken the noble route if he hadn't. It was a stupid choice, to be sure, but she understood that he was trying to protect her. He just wasn't giving her the benefit of making her own choices.

That was the problem.

That was the thing she didn't know if she could get over.

Liar.

Gideon might have pulled the trigger on ending things, but only because he'd beaten Lucy to it. She hadn't fought for him—for them. He'd tried to do the noble thing and, instead of telling him where to stick his high-handed attitude, she'd just walked away. So much easier to retreat than to put herself on the line and be rejected by him.

Lucy wove through the crowd of people on the corner and stopped next to the building, staring at the stream of yellow taxicabs. She'd projected herself. She couldn't even blame her history on her reaction. What she felt for Gideon scared the hell out of her. She *knew* he cared about her—loved her, even. They hadn't shared so much for it to be anything less than love. He wouldn't have told her to pick him unless he was one hundred percent serious. That wasn't how Gideon operated. He didn't play games.

Honesty. He demanded perfect honesty—and he'd given it, as well. She mentally played back everything he'd said to her. Nowhere in there was him telling her that all he'd wanted was sex. No, he didn't think he was good enough for her, so he'd cut her loose. *High-handed, but so very Gideon.* He'd chosen *her* happiness over *his*.

She needed to put herself out there. To tell him that *he* was her happiness. Lucy had lived a decent life the last couple of years. She'd been perfectly content, but she'd also cut herself off from anyone that would make her feel deeply enough to hurt her. She'd barely tried to date and hadn't attempted to reach out to friends she'd lost touch with.

She'd been the coward.

That stopped now. If Gideon didn't want her—didn't love her—he could damn well tell her to her face. That was the only acceptable reason for him dumping her. Anything else they could work past as long as they were together. Lucy would make him see that. The man might make her fumble her words a bit, but she'd power through it to get the truth out.

Her phone vibrated and she almost ignored it, but the only way to make her Dumpster fire of a day in court worse was to ignore a call from her client or one of the partners. But when she dug it out of her purse, it was the last number she expected to see there. *Roman?*

Lucy frowned and answered. "Hello?"

"I owe you an apology."

She blinked. This situation kept getting weirder and weirder. Roman had never called her before, and she couldn't think of a single reason he'd have to call her now. Unless… Her heart lodged in her throat. "Is Gideon okay?"

"What?" His shock seemed genuine and then he laughed, breaking her tension. "Shit, I guess I owe you two apologies. Gideon is fine last I saw him, which was yesterday. I should have realized you'd think the worst."

Lucy let loose the breath she'd been holding. "Okay. Sorry. I just thought…"

"Logical. I should have considered it." He cleared his throat. "Look, I fucked up, Lucy. I never asked your forgiveness for not telling you about Jeff, and then I went and compounded the issue by letting my guilt prod me to give Gideon some truly shitty advice."

She'd known that something had happened while Gideon was with Roman to push him into action, but she didn't hold it against him. Any of it. "Gideon's strong-willed. He wouldn't have been pushed into doing something he wasn't already considering doing."

"Still."

She smiled at the stubbornness in that single word. It was no wonder the two men got along so well. They were cut from the same kind of cloth. "Consider yourself forgiven."

"I'd actually like to make it up to you. Before you tell me it's not necessary, know that I realize it's not necessary and that's how good apologies work."

Amusement curled through her, though she wished he'd get to the point so she could hang up and call Gideon. "What did you have in mind?"

"What are you doing right now? A friend is doing a soft opening of his restaurant and I have a table reserved so we can talk."

"Right now?" She looked around. "I guess that works." Damn it, she wanted Gideon, but if she was going to get him to come around, it wouldn't hurt to have Roman on her side. Maybe she could use the lunch to mine for information. The thought buoyed her disappointment a bit. "Text me the address, please."

"Will do. I'll meet you there." He hung up before she could ask him any further questions.

Lucy frowned. *Strange.* Her phone pinged almost immediately and she frowned harder because she recognized the address. It overlooked Central Park, though it used to be owned by someone else. It must have cost a small fortune—or large one—to purchase. She set the information aside and stepped to the curb to flag down a cab.

The ride was blessedly short, all things considered. Lucy kept looking at her phone, but now that she was going to meet Roman, she didn't want to call Gideon until afterward. Just in case he wanted to talk immediately. Her stomach did a slow flip-flop. *Please be willing to meet with me.*

To her surprise, the restaurant was actually the top floor of the building. After getting off the elevator, Lucy stood in the entranceway for a solid thirty seconds, just taking in the opulence of the place. It screamed wealth with its polished white-marble floors and subtle gold accents. Nothing déclassé, but there all the same.

A well-dressed man strode over, a practiced smile on his handsome face. "You must be Lucy. This way, please."

She followed, taking in empty table after empty table. "I thought this was a soft opening?" Surely there should be *some* people there. *Good Lord, did Roman invite me here to shove me out a window?* She pushed the thought away. Hysterical was what it was.

"It is." He chuckled. "Just a *very* soft opening."

That wasn't an answer at all, but she allowed him to lead her into what appeared to be a greenhouse. The air warmed enough that she unzipped her jacket. Flowers of every color and shape lined the walls. There were even trees in the corners, which made her smile despite everything.

She was so busy looking at the foliage that she didn't realize the man had left—or that she wasn't alone—until she turned around and found Gideon standing in the doorway. Lucy froze. "But—"

"I'm sorry for the cheap trick. I wasn't sure if you'd agree to see me if I called." His dark eyes drank her in and she actually felt his longing even across the space between them.

Lucy shook her head. "Gideon, you have to *stop.* If you want to see me, call me and say so yourself instead of trying to manipulate things into a perfect setup." Now that she had him here, though, she was just glad she didn't have to have this conversation over the phone. She lifted her chin. "And if you love me, you stay. You don't choose the self-sacrificing route because you think you know what's best for me. You sit down and have a damn conversation where we talk it out."

His smile wasn't all that happy. "I fucked up."

"Yes, you did." She wasn't about to let him off easily, no matter how much she wanted to cross the distance between them and feel his strong arms wrap around her.

"I'm sorry. There's no good reason to explain why I freaked out, but guilt makes people do crazy things—like walk away from the woman they love because they think it's what's best for her."

"*I* decide what's best for me."

His dark eyes took on a tinge of sorrow. "I know. And we both know that I don't deserve to kiss the ground you walk on. Not because I love some idealized version of you, but because you're *you*. You're a good person, Lucy. The best kind of person. You are funny and kind and sexy as fuck, and I might not deserve you..." He took a step forward and then another. "No, I *know* I don't deserve you."

"Stop saying that," she whispered.

"Maybe we both fucked up. Fear makes for all kinds of mistakes, and what we have between us is wildfire." Gideon stopped in front of her and went down on one knee. "But, Lucy, I'd gladly spend the rest of my life burning for you." He withdrew a ring box from the inner pocket of his suit jacket. "I love you. I've loved you for six goddamn years, and I convinced myself that the right thing to do was to stand back and let you be with someone you deserved. I fought every single damn day not to pull some underhanded shit and steal you from that douche."

She reached out with shaking hands and touched the ring box. "Gideon—"

"I know you wanted a safe and pat marriage to some guy you don't give two fucks about. I can't offer you that, Lucy. But I can offer you a husband who will love you beyond all reason, even if he occasionally screws up. I can offer you a safe harbor, a full life and more sex than you know what to do with. I *am* offering you that."

She couldn't catch her breath. In all the scenarios she'd played out over the last few days, she'd never once imagined Gideon, down on one knee, offering her everything she'd spent two years being too terrified to admit she wanted. "Gideon."

"Yes?" He didn't look scared while he waited for her answer. He looked totally and completely at peace for the first time in as long as she could remember. As if he was exactly where he wanted to be—where he was meant to be.

Lucy stepped forward and tangled her fingers in his hair. "Steal me."

His dark eyes went wide. "That's a yes."

It wasn't a question but she answered anyway. "That's a hell yes."

He gave a whoop and shot to his feet, sweeping her off hers in the process. "I love the shit out of you, Lucy. I'll spend the rest of our life making up for six years of missed opportunity."

She kissed him with everything she had. "Maybe it

was good that it took us six years to get here and more than a few missteps along the way. There's a right time and place. This is *our* time and *our* place." Lucy kissed him again. "I love you, Gideon. So, so much."

He stepped back enough to slip the ring out of the box and onto her finger. It was…perfect. The simple silver ban framed a princess-cut diamond that was big enough to have her shooting a look at him. "Wow."

"Funny, that's what I say every time I see you." He pulled her back into his arms. "Wow. This woman is mine. And I'm hers."

"Yes and yes and yes." She smiled up at him. "Always."

* * * * *

Wanting more?
Read on for a sneak peek of
Katee Robert's next Mills & Boon Dare,
MAKE ME CRAVE.

Roman's story is far from over! He's got his eye on an up-and-coming business, but when the owner takes off on vacation, he follows her to paradise to convince her to sell. The only problem? He doesn't realize the gorgeous blonde he just met and the stubborn business owner are one and the same...

She made it to the restaurant with minimum fuss and found it practically deserted. Allie paused in the doorway, wondering if she'd misunderstood the woman who'd checked them in. Maybe it was closed?

"Looks like it's just you and me."

She jumped and spun around. The man stood a respectable distance away, but his sheer size ate up the space and made her feel closed in. She froze. *I'd recognize those shoulders anywhere.* As if to confirm, his gaze slid over her body as if reminding himself of what she looked like with nothing but what she'd worn on the beach. She tried to swallow past her suddenly dry throat. "You."

"Me." He finally looked her in the face, and she rocked back on her heels. The man was Adonis. There was no other way to describe his blond perfection, from his hazel eyes to the square jaw to the cleft in his chin to the body that just wouldn't stop. He might be wearing a shirt now, but the button-down did nothing to hide his muscle definition.

He held out a wide hand with equally perfect square fingers. "Let me buy you a drink?"

"We're at an all-inclusive resort."

His lips twitched, hazel eyes twinkling. "Have a drink with me."

Oh, he was good. Charm practically colored the air between them, and she had the inexplicable impulse to close the distance and stroke a finger along his jawline. To flick that cleft chin with her tongue.

Allie gave herself a shake. "Since we're the only ones here, it'd be silly to sit apart."

The look he gave her said he saw right through the excuse, and why not when it was pathetically flimsy? The truth was that this man was a magnet and she suspected she'd be drawn to him even in a room full of people. He waved a hand at the empty place. "Lady's choice."

"How magnanimous of you."

"I try."

She laughed and headed for the table in the middle of the small patio. There were half a dozen tables, and she picked a spot that put her back to the building and presented the best view of the ocean through a carefully curated gap in the foliage.

He eyed the view and then the chair across from her, and then picked it up and set it diagonally to her, rather than directly across. "Nice view."

She turned to agree—and found him staring at *her*.

Allie wasn't falsely modest. Life was too short to play games with body shaming and pretending she didn't have access to a mirror. She was pretty—beautiful when she put some effort into it—but her body wasn't the type someone would expect a gym owner to have. Sure, she had muscle beneath her softness, and she could keep up with the best of them in her spin classes, but she'd loved food just as much as she loved to sweat, and her curves reflected that. Some guys had a problem with that, though she didn't keep them around as soon as comments about "Should you really be eating that?" started.

This guy looked at her like he wanted to put her on the table and feast on *her* for dinner.

The desire stoked the flame inside her that had kindled the second she saw him. She leaned forward, checking his left hand. No ring. No tan lines to indicate there ever was one, either. "What brings you to West Island?"

"It's paradise, isn't it? Who wouldn't want to come here to get away from it all?"

That wasn't quite an answer, but she got distracted with the intoxicating way his mouth moved when he spoke. *Get a hold of yourself, Allie. You're in danger of panting.* She took a quick drink of water that did nothing to quell the heat rising with each second she sat next to him.

Luckily, a waiter appeared to save her from saying something truly embarrassing. He outlined the menu for the night and took their drink orders, and disappeared as quickly as he'd come.

They were in the middle of one of the most beautiful places Allie had ever seen, and she couldn't manage to tear her gaze away from this stranger. She licked her lips, every muscle in her body tensing when he followed the movement. She opened her mouth, but he beat her there, taking her hand and running his thumb over her knuckles.

The touch was innocent enough, but she felt that

light movement in places that were most definitely *not* innocent. She didn't have to look down to know her nipples now pressed against the thin fabric of her sundress.

His smile was slow and sinful and promised things she never would have had the gall to ask for. "This is going to sound unforgivably forward, but what do you say we get out of here and go back to my villa?"

It was crazy. More than crazy. She didn't even know his name, and she sure as hell didn't know anything more pertinent about him.

But there on the softly lit patio with the scent of tropical flowers and the soft shushing sound of the tide coming in, she didn't feel like Allie, gym owner and mother hen—the responsible one who could never afford to do anything crazy or make a misstep because too many lives depended on her.

Here, she was just Allie, a woman. A woman who desperately desired the man staring at her mouth as if doing everything in his power to keep from kissing her right then and there. She licked her lips again, secretly delighting in the way a muscle in his jaw jumped. "Yes."

"Yes?"

"Yes, let's get out of here."